THE GAP

JOANIE LUNSFORD

SHIRES ✿ PRESS

4869 Main Street
P.O. Box 2200
Manchester Center, VT 05255
www.northshire.com

THE GAP

©2019 by JOANIE LUNSFORD

ISBN: 978-1-60571-502-5

Building Community, One Book at a Time
*A family-owned, independent bookstore in
Manchester Ctr., VT, since 1976 and Saratoga Springs, NY since 2013.
We are committed to excellence in bookselling.
The Northshire Bookstore's mission is to serve as a resource for
information, ideas, and entertainment while honoring the needs
of customers, staff, and community.*

Printed in the United States of America

DEDICATION

Richards Street Gang

ACKNOWLEDGMENTS

Thanks to Catherine Rossi for being there from the beginning and all the help and support throughout. Thanks to Cheryl Blondina-Rabito, Sue Abdou, Robie Carlile, Mary Sierra, and Tracy Synowsky for reading my rough draft and offering suggestions and encouragement. Thanks to Krystal Lunsford for thoughtfully giving me her opinion when I bombarded her with questions. Thanks to Jimmy Lunsford for offering his ideas with such enthusiasm. Thanks to Bobby Lunsford for his support and encouragement during this process.

Finally satisfied with the content, I passed my manuscript onto my editor, Cathy Taylor, for much needed technical help. Thank you, Cathy, for that and especially for bringing to light my point when it got lost in my explanation. I deeply appreciate your conscientiousness to stay true to the spirit of my book. All the time, care, and attention you put into the work and gave me will never be forgotten.

Thanks to Debbi Wraga of Shires Press for book formatting and cover design. Thank you, Debbi, for taking both my visions and combining them to make a gorgeous cover. You have made my dream a reality, helping me share my voice on a topic that is often misunderstood and deserves compassion.

Last and most important, thanks to my husband, Jim Lunsford, for believing in me when I didn't believe in myself. You are my heart and my strength. I love you! I hope you know how much though I don't often say it.

INTRODUCTION

Triangles can be used to diagram life. A triangle has three points. Lives can be viewed in three periods of time. The three points can represent the past, present, and future. Upon reflection, insight is gained from the life we lived, life we are living, and life we hope to have. This grows and defines us by inspiring every decision we make, yet we cannot ever forget our point of origin.

It is this very origin I battle to escape from, but somehow keep getting pulled backwards. Might be a quirk in my personality brought to light, despair resurfacing from the drama of a relationship, or something witnessed triggering a flashback.

Can almost be like getting caught in an undertow. In too deep with a constant pulling. Swim furiously to get to shore, but the ocean has other plans. Efforts prove to be successful, though. Sand sticks to flesh while crawling up the beach. Turn around, stare at the raging ocean, and are faced with the knowledge, next time you just might not make it out. Call it a day, leave and never look back. The more distance covered, the better you feel. Become increasingly comfortable in your own skin as the sand begins to dry and flake off.

So true of the inner struggles fought in order to survive. Pushing forward is the only way out of being lost forever. Walk away, but never totally escape the feelings of uneasiness that have left emotional scars. Despite the effects creeping up every now and again, I am in a far better place. At least now, I have an identity.

1

WHO I AM

I was named Kerrie. I wrote my first book after high school and it became, as they say, a major motion picture. I packed up and moved to Los Angeles prior to filming.

My house was very comfortable, with two stories and five bedrooms. Mediterranean design, arched windows, and a dramatic porch with scrolled columns. An arched doorway entered into a foyer with more scrolled columns. Mosaic tiles on the floor and steps added touches of color and shine to earth-toned surfaces.

Plenty of room for company and entertaining. The living and dining rooms were an open floor plan. My family room was enormous and had a warming fireplace and built-in entertainment center. From the family room, living room, and master suite, double pocket sliding glass doors opened to a large veranda with wet bar, pool area, and pool house.

The pool house was fully furnished and could serve as a guesthouse. Very roomy. My favorite feature was a salt-water rock lagoon pool with waterfall grotto and elevated spa. Surrounding all of it was a beautifully landscaped lawn and outdoor garden that was artfully designed with lush green foliage and colorful exotic plants. Speaking of which, I had hired a new lawn guy who had yet to show. I'd been hanging around all day, attempting to work on my latest novel. No such luck, since I'd hit that proverbial wall of writer's block.

My friend Erin lived next door. Her place was very similar. It had been great having her as a neighbor. We dropped in on each other frequently to chat or when we needed to vent. This day was turning out to be one of those times when I needed to visit.

I went over to see Erin, entering through her sliding back door as I often did. Found her sitting in her kitchen drinking a cup of coffee. "What a waste of a day," I began. Helped myself to a cup and had a seat. "Having severe writer's block, and to top it off, my new lawn guy never showed." At that moment, my eyes were drawn to a hottie who had appeared in the doorway with nothing but a towel wrapped around his waist.

In a very sexy Italian accent he said, "So sorry, I was not aware you had company." He disappeared as quickly as he had appeared. My jaw dropped. Erin's eyes were wide with horror, fearing I might be pissed. She stammered out some classic line about how there had been some sort of accident and his clothes were in the wash. And, of course, a shower had been necessary. Sounded right out of a movie, her being an actress and all. With the way my day had been going, I busted out laughing. As did Erin. We sat there laughing hysterically for several minutes before I begged, "So tell me everything. And don't you dare leave anything out." Erin leaned into me and began…

———————

I was catching some rays poolside when a voice said, "Excuse me, but I rang your doorbell, and then heard music coming from back here." With the sun in my eyes and using my hand to shade the glare, I looked up. Standing in front of me was this gorgeous vision. Short dark hair, curls spiraling over his forehead, perfectly chiseled face, and the most beautiful hazel green eyes I've ever seen.

"Well, I hope you pardon my intrusion," said the vision. "My name is Davide, and I'm here for the gardener position." I knew Kerrie had spoken of hiring a new guy, but come on. Clearly, he was not aware of being at the wrong address, and this was like a gift I was not about to return.

After a brief pause, I commented, "Yes, have a seat, and tell me a bit about yourself."

"What would you like to know?"

"For starters, where are you from?"

"Italy. I worked at a hotel there. Part of the pool staff. Worked at landscaping for additional money, as well. Have not lived here long."

"Where are you staying, if you don't mind me asking?"

"At The Malibu Boarding House. Only had enough cash to pay to the end of the week, so I really need the work. I can, how do you say, be handy in other ways, too." *Bet you can be* was the caption above my head.

"Understand," I replied. "And as you can see, I have a pool house. It's fully furnished, and you are more than welcome to stay there for as long as you like." I stood up, walked to the door, and got the key from under the mat. As we stepped inside, a look of relief came over Davide's face.

"Thank you. Very kind of you. Don't know how I could ever express my gratitude."

"You just did." In his excitement he gave me a kiss, and I responded. Our embrace quickly turned passionate, and my bikini top slipped, exposing more of my right breast.

Davide touched the breast with one hand, while reaching behind my back with the other, and untied my top. I wrestled with the belt on his pants and unbuttoned them. They fell to the floor with my bikini top.

Arms stretched high, I yanked the shirt over his head. While lifting me up, he placed his mouth on a nipple. Being carried toward the bed, I felt the warmth of his tongue moving from one breast to the other as I ran my fingers through his hair.

Gently laying me down, he pulled my bottoms off, and tossed them aside. His tongue continued to explore downward, ending inside me. My whole body moved with a tingling sensation that took me over. Head slung back and fists clenched, I could not contain myself, and finally climaxed. I was totally moist, and once my body was still, Davide backed off the bed.

I watched as he slipped out of his speedos. Approaching slowly, he eased inside. Thrusting up and down, in and out. My body perfectly synchronized with every movement. I was immersed once again. We both came and collapsed into each other's arms, bodies entwined. Consumed with exhaustion, but at the same time feeling so alive.

———————

Once Erin finished, I instantly said, "Wow! Can't very well say TMI since I told you not to leave anything out." We both giggled as I fanned myself.

Erin asked, curiously, "What happened to your previous lawn guy?"

"Funny story, actually. At least it is now. And pretty ironic, too, considering. In short, I slept with him. We both knew immediately it was a mistake, as the thrill left and was replaced by guilt. Dillon was his name, and he had been seeing a girl he was just crazy about. I knew about it and felt bad."

"Why did you feel bad?"

"Don't remember exactly, but just did."

"You carry around a lot of guilt and really need to work on that."

"Do you really think so? I actually think I've raised the whole guilt-carrying to an art form."

"You know what I mean, Ker."

"I know. I know, Rin." We had given each other nicknames, as close friends often do. Terms of endearment, if you will. That's why I was the only one who could call her that. But only in private, lest her fear of being forever referred to as "Rin Tin Tin" came true. It was the name of the dog from a TV series we had heard of, a beautiful German shepherd. "Anyway, I should thank you for saving me, in a way."

"How so?"

"Well, I've been holding off on a replacement until my raging hormones are in check. Thought they were, but I know now they are not. I'm leaving to go jump in my pool. Feeling a need to cool off. See ya."

"Bye then, and love you."

"Back atcha." On my way back, I became reminiscent of the day we first met. It had been at Universal Studios.

2

FIRST ENCOUNTERS

It had been the big day. I'd just arrived at Universal Studios. My agent had even sent a limo to bring me. Once my book, *Misguided*, had turned into a movie deal, I was asked to collaborate on the screenplay. It was the first day of shooting, and I was supposed to assist the cast with character development.

The lead actress was an upcoming star who had gotten her start as a singer-songwriter. From what I'd seen, she seemed perfect for the part. She matched the description of the character's appearance.

The director spotted me and yelled, "Cut, be back in twenty." He walked over with extended hand and said, "You must be Kerrie Brannon. I'm Kirk Garrett." I shook his hand and was awestruck. He was very attractive, with sparkling blue eyes and shoulder-length brown wavy hair.

"Yes," I said, "I'm a big fan. I've seen all your movies. Some of them more than once." I rambled on, as I did when I was nervous.

Kirk smiled. "I'm very flattered, and am a fan of you, also. Your book is brilliant. Could not put it down until I read the last word. Knew immediately I must make this a movie, but wanted to stay true to the spirit of the book. So, thank you for coming. I'll introduce you to our female lead and then leave you alone to get acquainted."

I followed him over to a young lady in maybe her early twenties, with sandy blonde hair and dark brown eyes. She was pacing and appeared to be going over her lines. Kirk put his hand up to catch her attention. "Erin, this is Kerrie Brannon."

Erin reached out her arms for a hug, and said, "Nice to meet you, Kerrie. I'm Erin Corta. Your name is very familiar to me. Wait, why do I know that name? Have we met before?"

"No," I replied, "I don't believe so."

She stared at me in deep concentration and finally said, "I got it. Used to live near you when I was a kid, and then my family moved away. You don't remember me, do you?"

Now I was the one in deep concentration. "I'm sorry, but Corta is not ringing any bells."

She grabbed my elbow and moved me to a private spot. "Corta is just my stage name. I was known back then as Erin Vista."

I screamed with delight at the memories that surfaced of a simpler time. A life from so long ago, but never forgotten. "I absolutely remember you, and am flattered you remember me."

"Of course I do. I know you and your mom moved in with your grandfather after your dad left. This wasn't long after we moved away. Also, I was sorry to hear of your mother's passing."

"Thanks, Erin. A lot of time has passed since then. I try not to think about it much."

"Understand. I also know your grandfather is from Ireland, and was told you're named after the county he's from. Always thought that was cute."

"Cute, all right," I said, "if that were true. Actually, my grandfather owned a pub, 'Kerry's Pub,' which he named after the county. Story goes, my mother worked there in the evenings sometimes, to help out. She was also pregnant with me. Anyway, during closing one night, her water broke. Well, there was not enough time to get to the hospital. So you see, the pub is named after the county, and I am named after the pub. My mother just changed the spelling."

"I love that," chuckled Erin.

I grinned in response. "I actually do, too."

Erin was called back to the set, and we made plans to grab a drink later to catch up. Walking back toward Kirk, I saw him motioning me over.

"Before we get started up again," said Kirk, "I just want to let you know this is your picture as much as mine. So, don't hesitate to give your input."

"Thank you. Means a lot." Our conversation soon shifted from serious to witty. The banter between us was easy. Between takes, I caught Erin giving me a wink and thumbs up. A spark definitely existed. I knew it did for me, at least, but wasn't sure about Kirk. I couldn't read if he felt something also, or if he was just being friendly. Assuming the spark was mutual, whether or not it ignited a flame remained to be seen.

"That's a wrap," Kirk called out. "Let's reconvene at eight o'clock sharp." Kirk's mouth opened to speak to me at the same time his phone buzzed, and he looked down to see who it was. "I'm sorry, but I have to take this. See you tomorrow, Kerrie." I waved goodbye and heard Erin calling me.

"Hurry up, I've got just the place for our drink. Go there every time I tour in town. Do you have your car here?"

"No. A limo dropped me off. Compliments of my agent. The driver said he would stay in the area. He has a classic surfer dude look, but I cannot remember his name. I'm sure he told me. He wrote his number on a card and told me just to call when I'm ready. Wait! Maybe he wrote his name down as well." I quickly removed the card from my purse. "Drat, no such luck." I made the call, and it was not long before the limo drove into sight.

The driver got out, tipped his cap, and, as he came around to open our door, asked, "So where we heading tonight, ladies?"

Erin promptly spoke up. "Sunset Boulevard. The Twilight Club. And thank you."

"Yes, I know the place, and my pleasure." When we reached our destination, the place was hopping and clearly very trendy. There was a line from the entrance all the way down the sidewalk. As we approached the door, the bouncer looked our way.

"Nice to see you again, Miss Corta. We've missed you." Of course Erin had connections.

"Thank you, Tony. I've missed all of you, too. Let me be the first to introduce you to Kerrie Brannon. She wrote *Misguided*."

"I'm not much of a reader, but I assume there's a connection to the movie being filmed in town."

"Her book inspired the movie."

"Pleased to make your acquaintance, Kerrie."

"Likewise, Tony."

Tony stepped aside and motioned us in, then yelled out, "Hey, guys, look who's back!" There was a tremendous cheer from the crowd. Again, I wasn't surprised. Erin had a winning personality. "Oh, and congratulations on your success, Miss Brannon. Don't be a stranger."

"Appreciate it Tony, and I won't."

We entered and made our way to the bar. "My treat," said Erin. "What will you have? I insist," she interjected, before I could utter a single word. My face must have shown I didn't feel comfortable letting her pay. It was always easier for me to give than to receive. Didn't know why, exactly. My reaction was related to a feeling I immediately got, without any conscious reason behind it.

"A pint of draft beer from a local brewery," I said. "Bartender's recommendation."

"I'll have the same." Erin lifted two fingers, signaling the bartender.

"What can I get ya, Miss Corta?"

"Two pints of your best local brew, Shane"

"Absolutely. Coming right up."

"Thanks Erin," I said.

"Don't mention it. Do you remember Ashlyn Balsamo?"

"Yeah, I used to hang out with her sister Haley."

"Right, I remember. Well, Ashlyn and I have stayed in touch. She is going to flip when I tell her about you." I smiled from the images of good times. "So, tell me about yourself. Did you always want to be a writer?"

"Pretty much. I read a lot and loved becoming part of the story. Intrigued with becoming the storyteller, but I was done with school once I graduated. To be perfectly honest, was done with school before I was done with school. Loved reading psychological thrillers by Devlin Scott. Devlin is a local author who recently retired, but he was leading a writers' workshop. As luck would have it, he also frequented Kerry's Pub, and my grandfather used his charm to get me in. I would attend the workshop in the morning, then spend the day writing in the apartment above the pub, which is where we lived. At night, I worked in the pub. This is the book, and here I am.

"Love all your music by the way. Your lyrics really speak to me. The connection I feel with your songs made it seem like I knew you. I'm sure you get this all the time, but it's crazy I actually do know you, and I'm thrilled. Your turn."

"Thanks, and I'm thrilled too. To start, I felt the same way about school myself. Formed a band with some friends after high school, and we played gigs all around town. Finally caught a break after one of our performances was signed and made it on the radio. We recently toured around, and Los Angeles was our final stop. The night of our last performance here, Kirk came back stage and offered compliments of the show. Asked me if I ever considered acting, because he was casting for his latest movie and had a part perfect for me. Sounds like a pick-up line, doesn't it? But it wasn't. It's been strictly business. So I guess we both owe Kirk for our reunion. You two seemed to hit it off."

"Well, he is awfully cute. Do you live around here?"

"Currently living with friends, but I need a place of my own. They are driving me fucking crazy. Actually, I'm looking for a house with a pool. Seeing as I'm going to be here for a while, looking to relocate from New York. Will probably keep my condo, though, because I'll have to go back intermittently to record my music. Familiarity with the studio and all. Love all the guys there."

"Are you serious? I mean about looking for a house."

"Yes. Why?"

"The house next door just went on the market. You *must* be my neighbor." I wrote down the address and placed it in Erin's hand.

"Sounds great. Being neighbors would be so much fun. I'll check it out tomorrow. Better get home now and get some rest."

"Right. I'll call my driver. I hate not being able to remember his name. Oh well." I rummaged through my purse in search of a buried phone. After making the call, we made our way through the crowd toward the exit. "Wesley," I blurted out.

"Excuse me?" asked Erin.

"The driver's name. It just popped into my head. Crazy how the mind works."

"I know exactly what you mean." Wesley was waiting right where he'd left us. He took Erin home, and we said our goodbyes.

3

SPIRITS

I'd been enjoying lounging on my veranda after my swim. Must have fallen asleep, since I now found myself waking up. I stood up, stretched, and gravitated toward the wet bar. Grabbed a glass, removed some ice from the bucket, and dropped the cubes in. There was something appealing about the clink as the ice hit the glass. I'd started to pour in some rum when I heard Erin's footsteps on my veranda. Laughed out loud, recalling my visit with her earlier.

"Can I join you?"

"You know it. What can I get for ya?"

"Whiskey on the rocks."

"You got it. I was just laughing about you stealing my lawn guy."

"Yeah, crazy mix-up. Now I have to let my current lawn guy go. Unless you want to hire him, or I'm willing to share. Sharing is what friends do, ha ha."

"Quite all right. I'll hire your previous guy." Having an evening drink together had become a daily routine. But I knew it was just an excuse Erin used to check up on me since my break up with Kirk. "I've been meaning to thank you for taking care of me."

"No need, but don't you ever scare me like that again. Promise me, Ker."

"Promise, and I know it's why you've been coming over. You're not fooling me. Fess up."

"Okay, it's just you're like the little sister I never had. I want you to be fine."

"I am, Rin. Truly I am. Thought you were in New York. How did you find out?"

"I was. Got home around five o'clock, and Kirk called me." I could tell from Erin's eyes her mind had drifted off.

———————

I had just stepped in the door and was greeted by my phone ringing. I saw it was Kirk and answered. "Hey."

Barely got that out before he blurted, "Have you heard from Kerrie lately?"

"No. I literally just walked in the door. Why? What's up?"

"She popped in earlier, and let's just say, I was not alone."

"You fucker."

"Look, Erin, I feel bad enough, and besides, it didn't mean anything."

"Really, are you seriously going to go with that line?"

"That is exactly what Kerrie said. I have been trying to reach her ever since, and she won't pick up."

"I can't believe you thought she would after that. You are an asshole. How long ago was this?"

"I don't know. A while ago. Will you just go see if she's all right?"

"Yes."

"Great, and please have her call me."

"Well, that's not going to happen. The best thing for Kerrie is to forget your sorry ass, and she probably already has." I hung up. I was cool on the outside with Kirk, but frantic on the inside.

Kerrie has a huge heart, filled with love, which fuels her compassion. This is what she clings to for strength. However, she also has an intense sensitivity, feeling everything to the extreme, which is her vulnerability. And this makes her fragile and causes me worry.

I raced over to Kerrie's and barged in, shouting out her name to no response. My heart stopped as I entered the family room and saw all the empty beer bottles lining the floor. A shot glass and a bottle of tequila were on the coffee table. Apparently, my concern did not prove unwarranted. Just outside the master suite was Kerrie, sprawled out on the floor. I let out a scream. "Kerrie!" Shaking her, I kept repeating, "Wake up, it's Erin."

Finally, without opening her eyes, she grunted, "Leave me alone, Erin." And then slurred, "You don't understand."

"Yes I do," I said, before she passed out again. I put her arm around my neck and stood up. Got her to the master bath and propped her up against the toilet, knowing full well what was coming next. Been there, done that.

Quickly grabbed some washcloths from the cabinet above and turned on the sink. Soaked them in cold water, placed them on her forehead, and kept waking her up. What followed was predictable. A repeating cycle of her waking up, heaving in the toilet, and passing out. After what seemed like an eternity, Kerrie's eyes were finally able to stay open. Looking up and seeing me through fuzzy vision, she spoke with a hoarse voice. "Erin, is that you?"

"Yes, sweetie, it's me." Kerrie usually had such a nice tan, but now she looked so pale. "Welcome back," I said. But it was obvious she wasn't. She had no recollection, but I imagine the smell of vomit combined with booze helped her surmise the previous events. Embarrassed, she put her head down. "Look," I said, "before long we will reflect on this and have ourselves a good laugh. I promise. Now take a shower. You'll feel better."

Kerrie glanced up. "Why are you helping me?" Seemed like a stupid question, but I knew she asked it because she was lost and desperately needed to be found. A sadness was set deep in her eyes. Broke my heart.

"Cannot believe you are asking me this. You're my friend and I love you. You would do the same for me." Those must have been the magic words, because a twinkle was in her eyes again. Now, she was back.

———————

It was a long while before Erin looked at me. "Where'd you go?" I asked.

"Oh, was just remembering. Do you want to talk about it?" I didn't really, but could tell she wanted me to.

"I remember going over to Kirk's to surprise him, and ended up being the one surprised. Could not get out of there quick enough. Heard Kirk calling after me, and then felt my arm being grabbed. I turned abruptly around and snapped, 'Don't fucking touch me.' He told me it didn't mean anything. 'Really, are you seriously going to go with that line?'" I asked. Erin roared with laughter and spit out her drink.

"Kirk told me the same thing, and I responded with the same exact line."

"Too funny," I chuckled.

"Sorry. Continue."

"Okay. Got home and headed directly for my medicine cabinet of booze. Seems more appropriate than liquor cabinet, since I planned on self-medicating until I was numb. Must have blacked out, 'cause I can't recall much before you said the words 'friend' and 'love.' And that I would do the same for you. It was the reminder I needed to get back to myself. I vowed not to get this low again.

"Every time I fall into despair, it's deeper and deeper. Get scared sometimes I won't be able to find my way out." These thoughts had actually drifted away from me this time, and I had unwittingly spoken them out loud. Realizing what I had said, I moved to strike the last statement by lifting my glass and making a toast. "To friendship."

Erin lifted her glass and concurred, "Cheers," before drifting off again. I didn't know if it was the booze or the thoughts and memories creeping into our minds that kept interrupting the evening. No matter. I refilled both our glasses and waited.

———————

Kerrie sometimes alluded to her past. I could tell by her expression and quick reaction upon realizing it, it was always unintentional. Like tonight. She always followed by abruptly changing the subject. Probably in an attempt to erase the comments from my mind.

Anyway, I assumed it had to do with her mother. She only ever mentioned her one time, which I found odd. And it had been in connection with her birth. I was curious, but not enough to ask. Always felt this was private territory, not to be trespassed on.

———————

Erin lifted her glass again. "To being there for each other."

"I second that."

"Thank you, and good night, Ker."

"Good night, Rin." As she walked away, I yelled out, "Hey. When is Davide moving in?"

"Saturday," Erin replied, as she kept on walking. Right, Davide was paid up to the end of the week, I thought to myself. I then spotted Erin raising her hand to give a backwards wave.

The evening had proved to be quite cathartic for me. I'd actually been able to speak about Kirk without wanting to throw something. I cleaned off the wet bar and stepped into my family room. Collapsing on my sofa, I recalled our time together.

4

AN INVITATION

Filming had wrapped up the day before, and I had been thinking about the experience, especially my attraction to Kirk. My phone began ringing, interrupting my thoughts, and I saw it was Kirk. It was the first time he'd called, because we were, after all, previously spending our days together at the studio. I felt so giddy, it caused me to delay answering the phone. "Hello," I finally answered, attempting to sound nonchalant.

"Hey Kerrie, Kirk here. I'm heading out to get a bite at Dineros. Do you want to come along?"

"Sure." Dineros was casual, which clued me in on how to dress.

"Great, see you shortly."

"Okay then. Bye." I was sporting sweatpants and a t-shirt. My hair was in a ponytail that came out the back of the baseball cap I was wearing. No time to waste. I promptly took a shower and changed. Slipped into a white skort and bright yellow blouse. Slightly dried my hair so the wavy strands could dry naturally and not frizz. Applied eyeliner, mascara, and lip gloss, and was good to go. Needed no additional make-up, since I had a really nice tan. Was pretty proud of it, although everybody I was in contact with was tan. Stepped out of my room and faintly heard the doorbell. Slowly made my way to the door, because I didn't want to appear anxious. Grabbed my purse off the little side table at the entrance and opened the door. Kirk just stood there gazing at me.

"Excuse me for staring, but you are beautiful. Are you ready?"

"Thank you," I said with a smile. "And yes." Kirk looked fine, wearing a fitted blue shirt and jeans. He took my hand

and led me to a fire engine red Camaro. Then released my hand and scooted ahead so he could open the passenger side door for me. And when we arrived, opened my door and held out his hand to assist me. Quite the gentleman.

We were seated at a private table in a secluded corner, per Kirk's request. A server soon appeared with a basket of chips and salsa. "Good evening. My name is Sam. What drinks may I get started for you?"

Kirk answered Sam's question with a question. "What would you recommend, as far as sangria?"

"We have a magnificent house blend I would strongly suggest."

"Thank you, Sam. Could you possibly bring us a carafe?"

"Certainly, and may I interest you in any appetizers?" Kirk looked to me to answer.

"Just some cheese dip. Without jalapenos."

"Will do." When Sam returned with the carafe and cheese dip, he asked, "Are you ready to order?"

"Actually," Kirk said, "we are going to sit here and talk for a bit. But don't worry, I will take care of you."

"Of course. Take your time." The waiter walked away.

"So, Kirk, how did you become a big time director?"

"As you probably guessed, I'm a huge fan of psychological thrillers. Read all the Devlin Scott novels and aspired to make films in this genre. My uncle, Troy Garrett, was a director at the time. Had his own production company, Heartland Films. Have you heard of him?"

"Actually have. Romantic comedies, I believe. Many with Jenny Richards and Nick Rizzo. Quickly became America's favorite couple."

"Yes. Anyway, I was a senior in high school. Spoke with Uncle Troy about my desire to become a director, as well, and he invited me to come live with him after graduation. Actually, he and my Aunt Paula owned a restaurant, which had an apartment above it. Moved here that summer from Colorado, and that is where I lived. Been here about four years."

I could not believe the parallels in our lives. Interest in the same genre, not so much of a stretch. But out of all the authors, Devlin Scott. Then to have lived in an apartment above his family's business. Unbelievable! It was as if I were an open book he was reading, but he had changed the details ever so slightly to make it his own story. "I presume your uncle showed you the ropes."

"I'm sorry. Guess I jumped ahead. Tend to do that a lot. The answer is yes. I apprenticed under him. It was actually a win-win situation."

"How do you mean?"

"My uncle was looking to retire so he could focus full time on the restaurant. Uncle Troy was actually training me to take over for him. Started out directing scenes, and within a year I had progressed to directing a whole movie. Well, now you know my story. I'm anxious to hear yours."

"Our paths are very similar. My grandfather, Barry Flynn, owned a pub. And we lived in the apartment above. I, too, am a fan of Devlin Scott, and the summer after I graduated, he was offering a writers' workshop.

"Devlin lived within walking distance of the pub and was one of our regulars. Came in one afternoon with a handful of flyers and asked if he could leave them for anyone interested to pick up. I was interested, but could not afford it. My grandfather must have noticed an expression of disappointment as I picked up a flyer. He called Devlin over, but I don't know what my grandfather said to him. They had a brief conversation, and shortly after, Devlin told me he was looking forward to seeing me in his workshop. Figured my grandfather had used his Irish charm." Thought back to the extreme excitement I had felt in hearing those words. "From the workshop came the book. Took about a year to get published, and another year brings me to here."

"That's wild. You actually attended Devlin Scott's workshop. What was he like?"

"Very down to earth. Did not exude an ego about his success. Recently retired, but still very passionate about the writing process. This was the basis for the workshop. Devlin is extraordinary and his wit captivated the room." The memory of his wit struck a chord, which released a giggle. Kirk's look switched from intrigued to inquisitive. Like he was being left out of a private joke.

His curiosity got the best of him, and he jumped in. "I'm supposing you recalled something amusing." I knew this statement was more of a question, so I explained.

"Devlin gave us a project to come up with a concept we could build a story around. I was feeling pressure as I looked around the room at hands moving steadily across laptop keyboards and words flying up on the screens. That I truly wanted to impress Devlin did not help. I probably had a road map of frown lines spread across my forehead, and my eyes probably revealed my deep concentration at coming up with something. At this point, anything.

"The end of the session arrived. I noticed Devlin heading over, and in an attempt to avoid a blank screen, I jotted down a few points. It was crap. Pure drivel. I felt Devlin's hand resting on my shoulder as he leaned over to read. What followed was a very witty expression, which was not only helpful, but also proved a useful tool. He told me stories are not something that can be pulled out your ass, but rather thoughtfully received from your mind." Kirk and I shared a hearty laugh.

"That's great," said Kirk.

"Yeah. Devlin went on to say I needed to relax and allow the creative flow to take hold of me. Then, and only then, could the writing process begin. I apologize for going on forever."

"You didn't, and besides, the lead-in added to the humor. This is what makes you a gifted writer. Seems to me Devlin was the trigger you needed to tap into your creative side and release the gift you possessed all along."

"Nicely put." Kirk responded with a pleased grin.

"Appreciate the compliment. I want to talk about your book, but would like to save that conversation for our next date."

"This is a date!" I exclaimed, and babbled on. "I mean, I did not want to presume, lest I became disappointed. Well, an invitation to come along doesn't exactly signify a date. Like, say, asking me to join you would." Kirk busted out laughing, and I realized my nonchalant cover had been blown.

"You are absolutely right, which is why I intentionally phrased it that way. I was saving myself from feeling crushed in the event you said no. The date designation came from your response, not my question. Seems we both were protecting ourselves." We shared a moment of laughter again. Kirk's own admission made me feel better. After a few minutes, Kirk asked, "Shall we order?"

"Yes." I felt a connection to Kirk, a connection that had not existed with any guy I had dated previously.

The evening ended with a sweet kiss at the door and an invitation. "Would you join me for lunch tomorrow at my place? Does that sound better?" Kirk had a huge grin on his face.

"Much," I chuckled. "Sounds nice. Can I bring anything?"

"Just yourself. Oh, and a bathing suit. We'll go for a swim after."

"What time?"

"Is it okay if Wesley picks you up around one o'clock?" At that moment, a revelation popped into my head, and my response clearly expressed my surprise.

"Wait! Wesley is your driver?"

"I'm sorry. I thought you knew."

"No. I had no idea. My agent informed me a limo would be my transportation to the studio. Come to think of it, he didn't actually say he was sending the limo. Guess I just assumed. Anyway, thank you, and see you tomorrow."

"See you tomorrow." Kirk waited until I stepped inside before leaving.

I went to bed feeling happy about the evening and imagining what the next day would bring.

5

LUNCH

On the day of the lunch date, I spent all morning agonizing over which bathing suit to pack, a bikini or a one piece. I wondered which, if any, implications either choice would make. I felt it best to stop the madness of my indecision and went with my preference. Bikini it was, but which color? I couldn't decide, so I lay them all on the bed. I closed my eyes and picked. Opened my eyes to find I was holding the black bikini, so I packed it in my tote bag along with a wrap dress, some lotion, and my favorite towel. I grabbed my sunglasses in their case and placed them on top.

Wesley arrived at exactly one. I opened the front door with my tote resting on my shoulder. "Good afternoon, Miss Brannon."

"Nice to see you again, Wesley. And please, call me Kerrie." Placed my tote on the ground beside me and reached down to get my sunglasses. I took them out of the case and put them on. Wesley picked up my bag for me, and we headed toward the car. "I thought my agent sent you, originally. How long have you been working for Kirk?"

"Since May. Kirk told me about the confusion this morning, and we both had a good laugh."

"Can imagine. I moved here in May, wanting to be settled a month before filming started."

"I know. I thought the timing was suspiciously coincidental." I fell silent for the remainder of the trip, as I began to wonder if it had been a coincidence at all.

"We're here, Kerrie." I looked at my phone to see the time. It had only taken twenty minutes to get to Kirk's. Looking out the window, I saw an extraordinary Mediterranean estate. Made a mental note that we shared similar architectural taste, but his house was on a much grander scale than mine, naturally. Wesley opened my door and handed me my bag. Kirk was waiting at the entrance. He already had on his swimsuit and a Hawaiian shirt.

"Impressive home, Kirk."

"Thank you. Even have a theater room."

"Of course you do." Though this quote was generally regarded as humorous, fear instantly struck my over-thinking brain. I was concerned that Kirk might have taken it the wrong way, making my words hurtful. I promptly followed up with, "I've seen your enthusiasm for directing and imagine the room probably serves to inspire. Much the same way sitting in my study surrounded by books inspires me."

"Exactly. Let's eat, and then I'll show you to a guest room to change."

"Perfect." I clipped my sunglasses to the inside of my top and followed Kirk into a majestic foyer, where I was warmly greeted by a member of his staff.

"Welcome, Miss Brannon. My name is Marie. May I take your bag to a guest room?"

"Yes, Marie. Nice to meet you. Easy name for me to remember, since it's my middle name."

"Lovely to meet you, too, Miss Brannon, and don't hesitate to call on me if I can assist you further."

"Thank you, Marie. And call me Kerrie." She gave me a friendly smile, and off she went. The tour continued across a spacious open floor plan that offered a breathtaking ocean view. To the right was a gourmet chefs' kitchen with custom cabinetry and stainless steel appliances. I could see the cook busily preparing our meal. We approached a decoratively set table situated before wall-to-wall windows. Kirk pulled out a chair for me.

"I could sit here all day and never tire of this spectacular view," I said.

"I'm enjoying my view, as well," responded Kirk. "You really do have classic starlet features, with your brown wavy hair, pale green eyes, high cheekbones, perfect nose and chin. The camera would love you. Ever consider acting?"

"No. More of a behind the camera gal. Although, I am deeply flattered." A man was approaching our table with a tray and a bottle of wine. When he reached us, Kirk introduced me.

"Julian, this is Kerrie."

"Pleased to meet you, Kerrie." Julian placed the tray in the center of the table and placed the wine in an ice bucket beside us.

"Likewise, and the lunch smells delicious."

"Thank you. It's called a California Roll, which is a sushi roll consisting of crabmeat, avocado, cucumber, rice, and seaweed. Hope you're not allergic?"

"I'm not. Sounds tasty."

"Great, and enjoy. I will leave you to it then."

"Thank you, Julian." Kirk poured our wine as I prepared my plate. I took a bite and my palate was pleased.

"This is excellent."

"Glad you're enjoying the lunch. Told you last night I want to discuss your book, but first, I have a confession to make. I mentioned about reading to the last word. Well, I actually read the end first. Always do that, because if I like how a story ends, then I can enjoy the journey of how the author gets there."

"Interesting premise. So, how did you come to read my book?"

"Well, being a fan of Devlin Scott, I wanted to make a movie of his first book. Contacted him, and he was in the middle of the workshop you spoke of. Anyway, we made plans to meet after the workshop was done, which we did."

"Wow! That would have been great. I never knew."

"I could tell you didn't from your story last night."

"I don't understand. What do you mean?"

"When I met with Devlin, I was told flat out he was not interested in any movie deals for his books. He went on to explain he was content with his career, and besides, he's now enjoying retirement. He continued by explaining how an author can describe a character, but it is the reader who brings them to life with their imagination. It is this relationship with the reader he values, and feared a movie would change all that."

"I can appreciate Devlin's concern about a reader's interpretation of the characters being lost to the actors portraying them. I still enjoy seeing the movie, though, for comparison's sake."

"Me too. I was confused as to why he had met with me then, and asked him."

"I understand, and also find it puzzling." Knowing Devlin the way I did, I found myself amused. He frequently took his sweet time getting to a point. A conversation with him was like being out with a Sunday driver, having a long way to go, but being in absolutely no hurry to get there. If Devlin sensed any hint of impatience, he dragged the conversation out even longer. Devlin enjoyed secretly toying with people in this way. Due to his subtleness, the object was never aware, rendering the act harmless and making it humorous to witness.

"Devlin reminded me about what he'd said regarding his lack of interest in a movie deal for his books. But he didn't mean he wasn't interested, and handed me your final manuscript. Your book was in the process of being published. I loved it immediately. Your narrative hooked me. Classic thriller, jam packed with surprises. I wanted to wait till the book was in print before you were contacted about the screenplay. Knew it would be an instant hit."

At this point, I was shocked and speechless. Kirk saw my expression and continued.

"Kerrie, I can see this is news to you, but let me explain. First, you need to know Devlin did not and does not want you to know this. That was made abundantly clear. I could tell from meeting with him he does not outwardly show his feelings. In fact, his face and voice showed no form of expression at all. Very witty, as you described, but extremely dry. Kind of makes him more humorous, in a way. I say all this to convey my suspicion that you have no idea how deeply he cares for you. Is this correct?"

"Well, let's just say I knew Devlin used his reputation and connections to circumvent the traditional hoops a first time writer has to jump through. Devlin took my manuscript directly to his agent, which bypassed the whole sending a query letter and waiting process. As far as his feelings for me, I just assumed they were related to my writing. You know, out of his love for the craft."

"I see," responded Kirk. "Devlin's feelings actually carry a deeper meaning than you realize. Devlin spoke with your grandfather one afternoon, while you were still in school. He told me how your grandfather believed in your writing. He informed Devlin that literature was your best subject, and that you didn't get just As on all your writing assignments but A pluses."

"True. I could see my grandfather's pride when he read my papers. I'm very curious as to where this is all leading."

"Getting there. Okay, so your grandfather saw how much you enjoyed Devlin's books, which inspired your desire to write. He spoke with Devlin about possibly mentoring you. Didn't know if this would be of interest to you, or even if Devlin would agree to it. Devlin was delighted. In fact, he had been planning on starting a writers' workshop.

"Turns out, he had actually been mentored and was looking to do the same for another young writer. Being retired, he was overjoyed at the prospect of his passion living on through an aspiring writer. This was the purpose behind the workshop. To jump-start a career, much the same way his was. So, when you picked up the flyer and heard your grandfather call Devlin over, they were actually acknowledging confirmation of your interest."

"What you're telling me is, I was in the workshop before I picked up the flyer."

"Well, only if you were interested, of course."

"Wow! I had no clue."

"Again, it was obvious from the sequence of events shared in your story. Not to mention you had to ask me how I'd come to read your book. Devlin saw himself in you, which brought back memories of being young with the same eagerness to get started. Seeing the promise in your ability to tell a story, he understood, without words, that having such skills is what compelled you to write."

"Very true. My eagerness to get started, though, was due to the fact I had been held back a grade. So I was nineteen when I graduated. This really bothered me, which spurred my interest in the workshop. Naturally, I was grateful for the opportunity, but didn't realize Devlin thought of me as his protégé. Thank you for telling me, and don't worry about me revealing I know.

"I adore Devlin and consider him family. His attention made me feel special, and his support has done wonders for my confidence. And what can I say about my grandfather? He never uttered a word. Just let me go on believing my assumption. He raised me and never ceased to have my best interests at heart."

"You're not very good in the assumption department," Kirk said, and we both chuckled.

"Agree. Guess it's a good thing I'm not a detective, like in my book." We continued to laugh. I knew Kirk was referring to the confusion with the driver and was curious as to how he'd come to hire Wesley, but I felt I'd had enough enlightenment for one day.

"I intended on asking you what inspired the story," added Kirk, "but got side-tracked during the conversation. Besides, I think I'd rather leave the answer a mystery. If you're ready to go swimming, I'll take you to your tote bag."

"Yes. Lead the way." I had plenty to think about and didn't know how I felt about it all. I could sort through it later—first, it was time for a nice swim.

6

POOL TIME

The guest room also shared the view of the ocean. I entered the connecting bathroom to change. It was impressive, and held a sit down vanity, whirlpool tub, and oversized walk-in shower with glass block and mitered glass window that overlooked an outdoor garden. I couldn't help myself, and had to check it all out. I changed into my bathing suit and wrap dress. I placed my shorts and top with my bra and panties in the dresser. Grabbing my sunglasses, lotion, and towel, I headed back to Kirk. A broad smile appeared on Kirk's face as he looked me up and down and up again.

"Do you like?" I asked.

"Very much. Let's go for that swim. Although, to be perfectly honest, seeing you looking so drop dead gorgeous, I have ideas other than swimming floating around. I will, however, stay true to my invitation."

"Keep up the flattery, Mr. Garrett, and who knows where this day will lead."

"One could only hope, Miss Brannon. One could only hope." Kirk placed his arm around my waist and escorted me through the house. We headed down a spiral staircase to a massive sitting area decorated with framed movie posters from classic thrillers. Kirk opened a door on the right to show me inside what was clearly his favorite room. I took a quick peek. It was a replica of being at the movies, complete with theater seating, lighting, and fancy molding.

"This is awesome, Kirk." I received a smile of pride. We exited through sliding glass doors off the sitting room, which also had wall-to-wall windows overlooking an infinity edge pool. The infinity edge appeared to merge with the ocean. The visual effect was absolutely awe-inspiring.

"Amazing!" I said. "I'm thrilled to be here."

"I'm thrilled to have you here, and your enthusiasm, among other attributes, excites me. If you know what I mean." I did, and was feeling the same way. It was becoming difficult to contain the urges emerging inside of me.

"Yes, and you're not so bad yourself. I have a weakness for men with blue eyes and curly hair."

"Do you, now?"

"Maybe you wouldn't mind helping me apply some lotion all over my body." I emphasized the word "all" and wore a playful expression.

"Absolutely. You are speaking my language. Love being helpful, that is."

I rolled my eyes at him. "Yeah, right. I'm sure that's what you meant." Kirk removed his shirt as I removed my wrap, and we hung them over a chair. I spread my towel over a lounge chair, kicked off my sandals, placed my glasses on a little table, and handed him the lotion. Kirk poured lotion into one hand and rubbed it with the other. He started with my shoulders, moving down my back and working his way around front.

"You look very sexy in your bikini and, I imagine, even sexier out of it. Just us here. Gave the staff the rest of the day off and nobody can see." He pointed out a path. "That path leads to my private beach. All of this property is private." Now, I was initially apprehensive, but also surprisingly excited. Kirk slipped his hands under my top and applied lotion to my breasts, caressing each one as he did. I was becoming extremely aroused and didn't notice my top very smoothly being removed.

The feeling continued to intensify as Kirk moved his hands down my body, sliding a palm inside my bottoms and rubbing. With the other, he eased them off. Standing there nude in front of Kirk was strangely liberating and, at the same time, exhilarating. The inhibitions responsible for my initial reaction that often restricted me were gone. Kirk continued down my legs to my feet. Cracking a smile, he handed me the lotion. "Your turn."

"It will be my pleasure to return the favor."

"I assure you, the pleasure will be all mine." Spreading some lotion between my hands, I started by massaging Kirk's back and working up to his shoulders, before moving to massage his chest.

From Kirk's chest, I made my way down to his trunks, sliding my palms inside, down his hips, and slipping them off. Covering every inch of his body, I looked up to see a very satisfied smirk on Kirk's face. He reached out for my hand, and we headed to the pool.

I released Kirk's hand and stepped gingerly into the cold water, then quickly dove in to get my body acclimated to the temperature, and swam to the opposite end. I smoothed my hair and rested my arms on the pavement. Kirk swam up behind me and wrapped his arms around me, cupping my breasts and pressing his body tightly against mine. I felt my hair being moved to the side and his mouth sucking on my neck, followed by a tongue tickling my ear. Kirk turned me around and looked into my eyes. "Let's get out and rinse off."

We exited the pool and entered the outdoor shower, where Kirk turned on the sprayer and me, as well. With his head bent, he wiggled his tongue on each nipple. Sliding a hand down between our bodies, he eased two fingers inside, hitting just the right spot.

"Oh yeah." My eyes closed and mouth opened in response to his touch.

Kirk's fingers began as a slow dance that quickened in pace. I braced my hands against the walls as my hips jerked upwards and legs stiffened to the itch spreading throughout my body. My breathing grew stronger and my hips automatically swayed with the rhythm, as the intensity of the stimulation kept increasing. I squealed out in delight, fighting to hold on as long as I could, but reached my peak.

My legs weakened and I began to fall. Kirk quickly caught me under my arms and stood me back up. Never before had I experienced such a euphoric high. My mouth remained open with lips slightly parted, making way for Kirk's tongue to glide into mine. We kissed with all the desire flowing through us. We took a breather and found ourselves in a cloud of steam.

"You've got me all hot and bothered, Kerrie." Kirk lifted me up, and I wrapped my arms around his neck and legs around his waist. I could feel his joy rubbing on me and saw his excitement expanding. He raised me up against the back wall and repositioned himself to fit inside.

He entered teasingly at first, and then completely filled me. The increasing frequency of the motion resurged my energy. Gripping Kirk's shoulders, I arched my back and neck, as my hips moved feverishly to every thrust. The temperature rose between us until we shared an instant release. I was spent and dropped my head onto Kirk's shoulder. He carried me under the sprayer, shut the water off, stepped out, and started walking. I was resting comfortably on his shoulder with my eyes closed, relishing the feeling of contentment.

I opened my eyes just as we moved into a spa connected to the pool. Kirk hopped out and made us some drinks at the wet bar. He returned with a couple of frozen margaritas. We cuddled up together, enjoying the warmth of the spa and gazing out at the ocean. There was no need for conversation. I was so peaceful, and I couldn't remember the last time I had felt this relaxed, if ever. The sunset was now upon us, and I caught a chill from the night air. My shiver broke the silence.

"Are you cold?"

"Just a little, but I'm fine."

"Wait here. I'll grab your towel." I watched as Kirk took off and retrieved my towel from the lounge chair, and then headed to a supply closet near the shower. He removed two blankets and headed back. "Now, let's see if we can warm you up." I got up and Kirk wrapped my towel around me. "Dry off a bit," Kirk said, before racing off again with the blankets. He removed two cushions and laid them together. Wrapping a blanket over them, he tucked the sides underneath. With the other blanket, he plopped on top, rolled on his side, and patted his creation for me to join him.

I hung my wet towel on a chair and then nestled in beside him. Kirk covered us with the other blanket and we snuggled. Lying on our backs, we looked into the dark night and observed the stars. "Are you feeling better?"

"Yes, I'm all warmed up now. Thank you."

"Sure. Glad to hear it." It was an absolutely perfect day that had led to a perfect evening.

7

SUNRISE

I woke up to the bright sun and its rays beating down. Looked over to see Kirk lying beside me with his swim trunks back on, just staring at me. "Good morning, beautiful," he said, in a chipper voice.

"Good morning yourself, gorgeous. How long have you been awake?"

"Not long. I've been enjoying my view again. I took the liberty of having your clothes moved to the cabana." The cabana was a hut complete with thatched roof. "Are you ready to get dressed?"

"Yes," I responded, as Kirk rolled over and got up. Wrapping myself in the blanket, I stood, and we walked toward the cabana. Not long after entering together, I found my clothes neatly folded inside my tote. I slipped behind a bamboo screen to get dressed and hung the blanket over the top. It might have seemed silly to be modest, but it seemed appropriate, since Kirk was already clothed. After reappearing from behind the screen, I handed Kirk the blanket, which he placed in a wooden storage crate that resembled a giant treasure chest.

"Could you eat some breakfast?" asked Kirk. "Figured you might be a bit hungry since we kind of skipped dinner."

"Yes, and you figured correctly."

"Great. After breakfast, Wesley can take you home." Kirk's abruptness made our whole time together feel like an "eat and run" scenario. I felt as if I had overstayed my welcome.

"Are you tired of me already?" I asked.

"Not at all, babe. Quite the contrary. I want to spend even more time with you. In fact, I was kind of hoping Wesley could take you home to pack."

"Pack," I repeated, with a questioning tone.

"Yes, I'd like us to get away together. I have a villa in Barbados, and my plane is fueled and ready to go. If you're interested, that is." I was so ecstatic that without thinking I raced over to give Kirk a hug and a kiss. "I'll take this as a yes, then," Kirk said, also questioningly.

"Absolutely! Barbados! Are you kidding me? Of course it's a yes." As we exited the cabana, I saw a member of Kirk's house staff placing our breakfast on a table. When we arrived at the table, Kirk again pulled out a chair for me. But my hunger had been replaced by my eagerness for our trip. Now the whole "eat and run" scenario appealed to me.

I took a sip of orange juice, placed a napkin on my lap, and removed the round, domed, stainless steel plate cover, which revealed a slice of baked French toast surrounded by blueberries and sliced strawberries. I cut off a piece and had a taste. I savored the flavor and was pleasantly surprised to find the texture similar to bread pudding. I was relieved, because my nerves were jumping with anticipation, and I doubt my stomach could have handled anything heavy.

"So, Kerrie," Kirk said, interrupting my racing thoughts.

"Yes, Kirk."

"I want to answer the question you didn't ask."

"What question?"

"About my hiring Wesley."

"How did you know?" I was surprised.

"Well, I deduced an inquiring mind is in a writer's nature."

"True, or Wesley filled you in on our conversation."

"That, too. Anyway, Devlin informed me you have a lousy sense of direction."

"Sounds like Devlin. Did he also mention my tendency to be always late?"

"Yes, that did come up, actually."

"Devlin was always amused by those issues of mine and kidded me incessantly about them. I appreciated him finding these traits endearing rather than annoying. So, you hired Wesley for me?"

"Yes, moving can be stressful enough. Besides, I can always use a backup driver."

"Well, then, I am grateful for your thoughtfulness."

"Glad to do it. Now for my question. You mentioned your grandfather owned a pub. Does he still?"

"My grandfather's youngest brother, Brian, now owns the pub. My grandfather needed help and asked Brian to move here to assist him. He was still living in Ireland at the time. Brian moved in with us, and my grandfather actually groomed him to take over. My grandfather was ready to hand over the responsibility of the business, but continued to hang out in the pub and mingle with the customers. At least until he became ill with pneumonia and never recovered. He died in his sleep the month before I moved here."

"Sorry."

"It's okay. I'm just grateful he lived to see the success of the book. After all, from what you've told me, my grandfather was a very integral part. And that was in addition to all the support and encouragement he had given me throughout the years. What about your uncle? Do Troy and Paula still own their restaurant?"

"They retired after my cousin, Sandy, graduated from culinary school. Passed the restaurant on to her."

"It's nice both businesses stayed in the family. Well, I guess I'd better get home to pack."

"Yes, and yes."

After finishing my meal, I went back to the cabana to fetch my empty tote. I then scurried around the pool to gather my belongings, slipped into my sandals, and raced off to meet Wesley.

8

AWAKENING

I felt my body being shaken and heard my name. I'd been in such a deep sleep I found it hard to open my eyes. I ended up opening just one and saw Erin hovering over me. "Great! You're awake."

"I am now. Erin, what in the world is so urgent that you're waking me up?"

"Well, you asked me last night when Davide was moving in. My mind's been racing ever since. I have got to get the guesthouse ready for him. We need to go shopping and pick up a few things."

"I'd be more than happy to help you, but you do realize it is only Tuesday."

"What's your point?" Obviously, Erin had worked herself into a frenzy and was beyond reason. There couldn't have possibly been that much to do, but whatever.

"Never mind. Guess I don't have one. Let's go shopping."

"Awesome! This will be fun."

"Why don't you make a pot of coffee and let me hop in the shower. I'll just throw on some clothes after and be ready to go."

"Will do." I didn't waste much time getting ready, and followed the aroma out to the kitchen. Erin handed me a cup, and I brought it up to my nose to take a good whiff. Loved the smell of freshly made coffee. I added cream and sugar, and in the blink of an eye, we were on the road.

"Hey Kerrie, why were you sleeping on your sofa?"

"Well, after you left last night, I collapsed there. With all the Kirk conversation, I fell asleep in the midst of recalling our time together. Two months of total bliss. I don't understand what happened. To be perfectly honest, Kirk still calls me. Just can't manage to answer. Still stings a bit."

"I understand, and know about Kirk trying to reach you. Since you're bringing it up, I've had something to tell you, but felt you weren't ready to hear. Perhaps you are now."

"What is it?" I asked, eagerly awaiting a response. I could read the hesitation on Erin's face.

"I've bumped into Kirk a few times, and each time he begs me to talk to you about calling him or at least answering his calls. Kerrie, he is an absolute wreck. Maybe you should let him explain. You did, after all, say you don't understand. I believe the only way you'll get the closure needed is through hearing him out."

"You're right. I know you are. Certainly, sleeping with my lawn guy was not the answer. I will call him."

"Good. Moving on to a brighter note, I heard from Ashlyn. Did I ever tell you how thrilled she was you and I reconnected?"

"No."

"Oh, thought I had. Well, she was and is. Anyway, Ashlyn is planning a neighborhood reunion. Trying to get the old gang back together again."

"What fun! Count me in."

"Consider yourself counted. And you are not going to believe this, but Tessa Foster bought your house. She is hosting the reunion." Tessa had grown up across the street. The news about one of the neighborhood kids purchasing my family home made me happy inside.

"That's wild! Love that the reunion is being held at the house I grew up in. Our neighbors turned the house into a home. Is there a date yet?"

"I wholeheartedly agree with the important role our neighbors played in our lives. No date yet."

"Something to look forward to, then."

"Absolutely." We arrived at the mall. Had a feeling from the determined look on Erin's face I was in for a shopping spree.

"So Erin, where'd ya want to start?"

"Was thinking 'The Soap Shop.'"

"I love that store. Always find it humorous how the employees offer to help. It's fucking soap. How much assistance can someone possibly need?"

"Maybe if you're looking for a specific scent, the employee can help narrow your search."

"Seriously, do you think there are many people entering that store with a specific scent in mind?"

"Not really, but it's possible. Just a thought."

"You're right, and now I feel bad about my comments."

"You were fine till my last comment. So, if you feel bad, then I will feel bad. Was just having fun with ya."

"I know. Besides, had nothing to do with you. Started out with something I found to be humorous and, as usual, blurted it out in jest. Then, as usual, began wondering if anybody would view my comments as being in poor taste, which resulted in my regretting finding the whole thing humorous in the first place. And you're being ridiculous, cause you feeling bad will not help me feel better. It'll just make me feel bad that you feel bad because I feel bad."

"I'm being ridiculous. You're worked up over the idea of anybody finding your comments offensive. And, yes, it will help. Since you would feel bad that I feel bad because you feel bad, you would feel better."

"True. We, for sure, are a couple of over-thinkers. One is bad enough, but put two together and it's downright insanity."

We entered the store and had begun to look around when we were approached by a woman wearing a nametag reading "Bonnie."

"What can I help you with?" asked Bonnie.

"Do you have coffee scented liquid soap?" I said. "Found myself enjoying the aroma this morning. I thought it would sure be nice to be able to experience the scent of coffee throughout the day. Without having to make it, that is."

"I agree, but don't believe we do."

"You don't believe so, but is it possible?"

"I will check and be right back."

"Thanks, Bonnie." I turned my attention back to Erin, who looked amused.

"See, you did have a scent in mind," said Erin.

"Not really. Literally, the whole coffee scent idea quickly came into my mind and out my mouth before my brain had a chance to comprehend it."

"Wow! Your mind would be a wondrous place to visit."

"I know, right. Get my best ideas spontaneously. Funny thing is, I hope Bonnie finds the scent actually exists. Better yet, I hope it's in stock."

"I seriously need to get you out more. Your brain is crying out for stimulation outside your house. I picked out a couple items. What do ya think?"

"Point taken. Guess I have become somewhat of a homebody lately." I did a sniff test on Erin's items. "Nice." We perused the remainder of the store, and Erin added to her collection. As we approached the cashier station, I saw Bonnie in my peripheral vision. Turning my neck in her direction, I could see she was heading my way, and was amazed to see her hands were not empty. Could it be?

"I found it!" Bonnie exclaimed proudly.

"Great!" I said. She angled the dispenser, and I reached out my hands for a sample. My nose immediately captured the tantalizing aroma of fresh coffee.

"Wow! That's a remarkable likeness." I rubbed some onto my wrists and dabbed a little on my neck. "Appreciate you finding it."

"Not a problem. Just glad I could help after you expressed such an interest." Bonnie reached into the pocket of her apron and pulled out another bottle. "Brought an extra to replace the one I used as a sample. Can I assist you with anything else?"

"I'm good, and I'll take both bottles. Thanks again, Bonnie. I will be back."

"Great! Best be getting back to the front. Enjoy the rest of your day."

"You, too." We checked out and paused outside the store.

"Okay, so I need to stock up on bathroom supplies," Erin informed me.

"Do you mean like washcloths, hand towels, and bath towels?" I asked. Erin's expression looked like a light bulb had gone on.

"Probably should get more of those. Actually, I mean the standard shaving cream and shaver. Plus, a hi-tech electric razor. Some of the most awesome manly smelling shower gels, which we just got. A bottle of Cool Water, my favorite men's cologne. Lastly, one of those electric, pulsating foot baths that you can put Epsom salt into for my honey's tired, aching feet after a hard day. Funny, did not even think about what you mentioned."

"Know what you mean. None of what you mentioned entered my mind. Clearly, you are much better at this."

"True. We'll leave after this list is complete. Then on to our next stop."

"Did you say *this* list? How many do you have?"

"A couple. Need to pick out some furniture."

"I'm almost afraid to ask, but like what? Just curious, since your pool house is already furnished."

"And this from someone who requested coffee out of all the scents filling the store. Well, for the outside, a cozy red wicker patio set with a big shade canopy Davide can relax on when he's off. Then, I want to get a new bed."

"What about the bed you have? And touché."

"Decided I'd rather have a waterbed for there."

"I can see that."

"Also planning on a pool table."

"Sweet! What else is on your agenda?"

"Stocking the wet bar with tons of delicious champagne and exotic beers. This will be our last task, but we'll eat before moving on from here."

"Great! I'm starving. Did you get any sleep last night? You've put a lot of thought into this. Love all your ideas."

"Told you my mind was racing."

"Sure did."

———————————

We finally got home around six. Spent all day shopping and managed to accomplish everything. I had had no doubt we would, with Erin's determination. All the furniture was set to be delivered before Saturday. Including the pool table.

My feet hurt, which reminded me of an old expression, "Dogs are barking." I marveled at the conception of phrases, the choice of words strung together in such a way to convey a point that resonated and was repeated and passed on through several generations. I sat down, removed my sneakers, and rubbed the bottoms. Sure was wishing I had one of those pulsating foot baths. Decided a hot bubble bath would also work.

First, I entered the kitchen to place my new hand soap by the sink. One bottle on each side. While I was there, I figured I might as well get a glass of wine to sip during my bath.

Upon entering the bedroom, I began peeling off my clothes, leaving a trail behind me, as I made my way to the bathroom. I poured a cherry blossom mixture into the running water. Once the tub was filled with suds, I stepped in, rested my glass on the edge, and sat down. My muscles were all thanking me. I was enjoying the quiet when I heard the phone ring. Figured if it were important enough, the caller would leave a message. Stayed in long enough to finish my wine, but fortunately not too long. I couldn't stand having wrinkly fingers and toes. With my glass in hand, I got out, reached for the robe hanging on the back of the door, and wrapped myself inside.

Out of curiosity, I walked over to my phone to see who had called. No listing and no message. The thought of calling Kirk popped into my head. Holding the phone might have been the reason. Decided I'd better call before I chickened out.

Hearing the ring tone brought on the feeling of butterflies fluttering in my stomach. Finally, Kirk picked up.

"Hello Kerrie!"

"Hey Kirk. Look, I know you've been trying to reach me, but I needed some time."

"I understand. So, did Erin talk to you?"

"Yes. Just today, actually. We were on our way to do some shopping, and she explained about seeing you and mentioned your conversation. Erin expressed she didn't feel I was ready to hear about it earlier. Guess my bringing up you calling me indicated I might be ready now. Told Erin I would call you, so here I am."

"I am so glad to hear your voice again. Would love to meet with you. Anywhere you'd like. Please! Just give me a chance to explain."

"Okay. What about Brewers Café'?" I loved that place. Perfect any time of day. Not only did they have coffee, but they also brewed beer. The brewery sat behind the café and was always experimenting with different flavors. They also baked the most incredible desserts daily. "Perfect! When?"

"Tomorrow. Say around four o'clock."

"I'll be there. And thanks, Kerrie."

"You need to thank Erin. She convinced me it would be a good idea to hear you out. See you tomorrow then. Bye, Kirk."

"Goodbye, Kerrie." I placed the phone back in its charger and stared at my empty wine glass. Would be a shame to leave it that way, and besides, I was in need of relaxing. I returned to the kitchen for a refill, and then went off to my study to select a book. I intended to curl up with the book in the sitting area of my bedroom. At least until I became sleepy.

9

JUDGMENT DAY

Four arrived too soon. Entered the café and noticed Kirk sitting at the last table. Once I reached him, Kirk looked up and asked, "Is this table okay?"

"Yes, but can we switch places? Don't like sitting with my back to the door."

"Of course. I'm glad you agreed to meet with me. Shall we order first?"

"Absolutely." We approached the counter to order when I heard a voice, and then saw a familiar face appear from behind the swinging door.

"Hi stranger. Thought I saw you through the door. What ya been up to, Kerrie?"

"Hey Jake. Been a little busy lately."

"Well, I sure have missed you. Never dull when you're around." I leaned onto the counter.

"So Jake, I've been meaning to ask if your brownies have an extra ingredient. Felt slightly stoned the last time I was here."

"And you don't think it was related to downing four pints?"

"Nope, definitely the brownies. Believe I could have eaten a whole pie. Don't get that from drinking beer."

"Is that so? Well, I doubt you would have had time to eat even a slice that night. You were kind of busy on the dance floor."

"You don't have a dance floor."

"Exactly! Would have thought we did with all the dancing going on. You started out by taking requests for the jukebox. Before long, everybody was on their feet. You sure got some moves." Jake looked at Kirk and then back at me. "We'll continue this conversation later. What can I get you both?"

"Yeah, right." I turned to Kirk. "Kirk, this is Jake. He and his brother Dale own the place. They're also known as 'The Brews Brothers.'"

"Cute. Nice to meet you, Jake."

"You too, man. So, can I interest you in some brownies?"

"Not today," I replied. "I'll have a pint of root beer ale and some chicken fingers."

"I'll have the same," added Kirk.

"Okay then. Have a seat and I'll get it right out to you." We returned to our table. Kirk began to speak as soon as we sat down.

"Look Kerrie, you may not believe me or even care to hear this, but I truly am sorry." He stopped and stared at me. I imagined he was trying to gauge my reaction, but in my numb state, my plan was to listen first and think later, making reading me damn near impossible.

"I'm listening. Go on."

"I have never met anybody like you before. Felt a spark from our first meeting and asked you out to see if my feelings would grow deeper, which they did. The more time I spent with you only served to strengthen those feelings. Always felt suffocated in previous relationships and ended them, but not with you. I never could get enough of you, which scared the hell out of me." The arrival of our meal interrupted us. I related to everything Kirk had said, except the scared part.

"My experience was mutual. Don't understand why you were scared, though. For my part, I enjoyed the journey our relationship was taking. Every moment was special."

"The fear of our relationship not lasting consumed me to the point it became difficult to relax in what we had. Drove me crazy and I sabotaged it. Guess I foolishly thought that would be easier than the hurt I would have felt had you ended it. Knew it wouldn't be me. I did not set out to sabotage, mind you.

"Needed to escape from the fear, which led to sex. Knew the possibility of you dropping by was good. I did give you a key. Thought at the time, my need was worth the risk. Having it end, before I got hurt, if you know what I mean. The cost of the escape turned out being even more unbearable. Life without you is far worse than the fear with you. I swear it only happened the one time and honestly meant nothing. Just want you to know and believe me, although I am aware that does not make it any easier."

"No, it doesn't, but I do appreciate you telling me. Erin was right. I told her I didn't understand what happened. She responded by telling me the only way I'd get closure was by letting you explain. You deeply hurt me, but the doubt gnawing at me was what prevented me from getting closure and moving on.

"I have played us over and over again in my head. I couldn't help but think I was responsible somehow. I kept going back and forth between analyzing whether I was clingy to questioning what we had. Did I just see what I wanted to see, therefore making the relationship one-sided? This is what I meant by not understanding what happened. I'm curious as to why you believed I would end it."

"Listen to me. You did nothing wrong. Beyond protecting myself, I did not think my behavior through to the hurt I would cause you. I'm sickened by the fact I hurt you. The look on your face continues to haunt me. Crazy how you end up hurting those closest to you, which is the last thing you'd want to do."

"Yeah. It's also crazy what people do in the name of protecting themselves, and then they get hurt anyway, causing their own pain."

"Right. Now to answer your question. I guess with all my doubts, I convinced myself you would end it eventually. See, you and I were so good together, I found it hard to believe our relationship was even possible, much less that it would last. Knew how I felt, but did not know if you felt the same way. Honestly, ours was the longest relationship I have been in. For me, there has to be a connection. Don't see the point continuing unless I foresee a future. I feel suffocated otherwise and, like I said earlier, always end it.

"Anyway, it was important to me from the start that no secrets existed between us. This is why I felt compelled to be open with you at lunch. As I said, a spark existed for me from the beginning. The connection was immediate. This I knew. Not knowing your thoughts caused me angst. Even so, if I was living a one-sided relationship, as you put it, I did not want to know them, which obviously quashed any questions I might have asked about your feelings."

"So, in order to save yourself from your fears being confirmed, you caused yourself more anxiety in not knowing. Like my point from earlier."

"Well, putting it that way makes it sound stupid. But yeah."

"Oddly enough, makes sense." On some level, I could relate, because it spoke to the insidiousness of doubt playing on insecurities. Or insecurities giving rise to doubt. Either way, it created a ludicrous situation. "Appreciate your honesty. Finally, I have closure. Now that you've explained, are you feeling better, and can you move on?"

"Actually, no."

"Why? Do you need something else from me?"

"Because I don't want to. Move on, that is. I realize I screwed up and don't have a right to ask you this." He fell silent.

"What is it, Kirk?"

"I was hoping you would give me another chance. I certainly understand if you say no and will always be grateful you met me today."

"Tell you what. I don't hate you anymore." I paused to gather my next words, which Kirk misinterpreted as my being finished.

"Well that's something, anyway," he interrupted.

"I wasn't done. What I was going to say was, well, I was hoping we could be friends. No pressure, and we'll see where it takes us. What do ya say?"

"Fair enough. I'd like that very much. Now I am better."

"Good!"

Kirk managed to smile with relief, and so did I. We finished our meal, but continued to sit and chat. The sudden sound of a brief, feeble whimper grabbed my attention.

A mother was coming from the restroom with her child. The woman had a tight grip on the young girl's arm. I wondered what the girl could have possibly done to warrant such a reaction. I recognized the look of rage in the mother's eyes, and related to the fear in the daughter's body language. She was grimacing. Helplessness choking out speech. Rendered powerless to change the situation even if there had been a desire to speak.

They briskly left. The scene burned into my brain and fused with a flashback. Tears were beginning to well up, and I was fighting to hold them back. I had to get out of there quickly. I stood up, threw money on the table, and raced out the door.

10

LEFT BEHIND

After Kerrie left so abruptly, I was perplexed and concerned. Not knowing what to do, I called Erin.

"Hey Kirk, how'd…"

"Kerrie just up and left."

"What did you do?"

"Nothing. We were hanging out and talking, then she got real quiet and left."

"Well, there had to be a reason. Something must have happened."

"All I know is, Kerrie suddenly went into a blank stare, like she was lost in her thoughts."

"Think, Kirk. What prompted her deep thinking?"

"I really don't know. Wait, there was an incident involving a mother and her little girl. Could this be it?"

"Possibly. What kind of incident?"

"Well, the woman was angry, and appeared to be holding the girl's arm rather tight. You're from the same hometown. What do you know about how she and her mother got along?"

"Honestly don't know. Kerrie is four years younger, so we didn't exactly hang out together. Our parents were close, though, but I never saw any interaction between Kerrie and her mom, since all of us kids mostly spent our time outside. You know, away from any parents. A close neighborhood that produced many happy childhood memories. Guess in a way we were insulated in our small town.

"All I know is, shortly after my family moved away, Kerrie's parents split. The house went on the market and her grandparents moved them into their place. Probably hoped the family home could provide some comfort to her mother.

"Later, my mom got word and passed on to me that Mrs. Brannon had died. Getting right to the point, that is all she said. As a kid, you accept what you're told. No need to question for details. The subject never was brought up again. Looking back on it now, the hush-hush nature does make it suspicious." I could tell by the silence that Erin was contemplating her last statement.

"Throughout the years, did you ever wonder about the cause of death? Aren't you the least bit curious?" I probed.

"No, never. Always believed the story of Mrs. Brannon's death should remain buried with her. Could not see any harm in that. Considered it like keeping Pandora's Box closed. Although, my curiosity has been piqued with getting to know Kerrie."

"Do you think it's possible harm has come to Kerrie?"

"I suppose. Kerrie keeps her past private, which would keep her pain locked deep inside. It's about time to finally release some of it, and I suspect she probably is. I'm going over to see her now. Thanks for calling, Kirk."

"Sure, Erin. Let me know how she is."

"Will do."

11

ON A MISSION

Entered through the sliding back doors leading to the family room. Kerrie was rocking back and forth in an overstuffed chaise lounge chair with her legs pressed up against her and arms wrapped around them, buried in tissues and crying hysterically. "Kerrie! What the fuck is going on? Talk to me." She stopped rocking in response to my voice and lifted her arms up, revealing tissues in both hands. Kerrie spoke through her tears.

"Look at me, I'm a mess. Kirk must have called you." She could barely speak from crying so hard. A hiccup sound filled the space between each word.

"Yes. He is concerned. Said you just up and left. What happened?" With that, Kerrie started to settle down and stared at me for a bit.

"Erin, I know you well enough to know you would not have allowed Kirk only one statement before coming over here. And you know me well enough to know I would not have just up and left, as you put it, without a reason. You would have interrogated Kirk to get the reason."

"I did." I tried to think of what to say next.

"And?"

"The only thing he could finally come up with was something about an incident involving a mother and her little girl. The woman was angry and appeared to be holding the girl's arm rather tight. That's how Kirk put it." I knew by Kerrie's change in demeanor I had struck the right nerve. Her eyes glazed over as she looked away contemplatively. "Come on, Kerrie. Don't shut me out. You have kept your past secret and pain deep inside for far too long. My suspicion about you releasing some of the pain was correct. Talk to me and let it all out." I plopped down on the sofa beside her chair and waited until she was ready to speak.

After a moment, Kerrie spoke with a quivering voice, a result of the flood of emotion she had unleashed earlier. She was still unable to look in my direction. "Well, the scene triggered an uneasiness in me, which conjured a flashback. Seeing the girl like that, I traveled back in time. Felt an immediate need to get out of there before the tears welling up in me flowed out. The incident actually started with me hearing a brief, feeble wailing. I gather Kirk didn't hear the cry, since he didn't mention it."

"Guess not, and I can understand the urgency. What did you see in your memory that was so upsetting?" Kerrie faced me without eye contact before she began again.

"At Universal Studios, you mentioned my parents splitting up and my mother and I moving in with my grandfather. Actually, it was my grandparents. Don't know if you knew this or if it even matters."

"I did know that. Only mentioned your grandfather because I remember him. I know your grandparents used to stay with you while your parents were away. Your grandfather was quite the character. See, he would often sit on the front stoop and call us older kids over to where we'd all sit around him. Loved hearing his soft brogue as he would crack a joke or tell us stories." In the midst of my recollection, Kerrie looked up to make eye contact.

"Ha, did not know that, but this was so like my grandfather. Always quick with a joke and could spin a yarn like nobody's business. Both told with a mischievous smile. I spent most of my time at the opposite end of our street. Basically just went home for meals and sleep. So, I was not aware he did that. Thanks for telling me."

"Certainly. Anyway, what happened? This has to do with after you moved?"

"Yes. My mom had taken me shopping. She wanted to pick out new outfits for me. It was a great day. We grabbed some lunch, and she even treated me to ice cream. Ordered me fudge ripple, my favorite, and requested a cup because I was cone-challenged.

"We were going to continue our shopping when we bumped into my mother's best friend, Hazel, from high school. I'll never forget her name. My mother introduced me, and Hazel looked down at me, smiled, and said, 'Hello Kerrie,' to which I politely smiled in return. Hazel then turned her attention back toward my mother and proceeded with the usual catch-up conversation. Goodbyes were exchanged, and Hazel crossed the street and shortly was out of sight." Kerrie paused and stared off again.

"Sounds nice. What was the problem?" Kerrie continued as if all the emotion had drained out of her.

"That's just it. Wasn't aware there was one, until my mother looked down at me with the same rage I witnessed at the café. She tightly grasped my arm and we moved hurriedly toward the car. I grimaced from the pain. Dared not cry out from fear of worsening the situation."

"You identified with the little girl, which brought you back to the time of a similar incident," I jumped in, wanting to clarify my understanding before we moved on.

"Exactly," Kerrie confirmed. "It was an excruciatingly silent ride home. The only thing obvious to me was our shopping had been cut short. We pulled into the garage and entered the house. My mother furiously turned the doorknob, and it was as if she had turned a knob on the radio from off to high volume. A blaring voice came from my mother's mouth. She began shouting at me at the top of her lungs."

"What about? And where were your grandparents?"

"They were working at the pub. The gist of the whole thing was that I had not verbally responded to Hazel. In my defense, I mentioned I had smiled. This was not good enough. I will now tell you the lessons learned that day. Smiling is not a sufficient response to a verbal greeting. My silence was rude and an embarrassment. The bottom line was I had apparently made my mother look bad in front of her friend. The anger she exhibited was paralyzing."

"Wow! How old were you?"

"I was ten with no reference point, therefore lacking the reasoning skills and insight offered from wisdom. Kids have no concept of irrational behavior and believe the words of a parent are fact. My mother told me I was rude, so it must have been true. I can look back now with more clarity."

"How so?"

"I can see my mother's reaction was extreme. And perception becomes reality in a world where appearances are everything, breathing life into the assumption everyone views situations alike, one side to every story. Do you know what I mean?"

"I think so. Your mother felt your silence was rude and believed Hazel must have thought so, too, which reflected badly on her."

"Yes. The fact I was a kid and possibly shy in the presence of an adult I didn't know did not compute. Doubt Hazel even took notice. In reality, she probably did find my smile sufficient."

"I agree. What happened to your mother? I was simply told she died."

"Really? I figured everyone knew."

"Yes, really, and no, since I didn't have a need for details. But knowing you now has made me curious. I understand if you don't want to talk about it."

"No, it's fine. A car accident. After we moved, my mother could not cope. Spent most of her days in bed with booze and pills. On rare occasions, she got the fancy to go out. Like the day she took me shopping."

"I can see now the significance of you calling it a great day."

"Yeah, but there's more to it. Won't get into all that now. Anyway, this particular day my mother came downstairs all dolled up. I was in middle school at the time. She looked so beautiful, and you would not even suspect she was having any difficulties. Looked ready to hit the town."

"Party it up, so to speak," I said.

"Exactly. Well, I was out front catching lightning bugs when a police car showed up and parked right in front of the house. The officer got out and approached my grandfather. He was, as you put it earlier, sitting on the front stoop. I just stayed where I was so as to not interfere with adult business, which had been a lesson ingrained in me. The last thing I saw was my grandfather putting his head down and then looking in my direction. He called me over as the officer was leaving. Well, you can pretty much take it from there. I'll never forget that sinking feeling as I made my way up to him."

"That's awful. So how did you come to live at the pub?"

"After my grandmother died of a stroke due to a brain aneurysm, the house became too much for my grandfather. He sold the house and used the money to expand the pub and the apartment above. Makes perfect sense, since running the pub was enough to keep up with."

"Kerrie, you have stored this pain for years. It's about time you had a release."

"I suppose you're right. The memories remained, but I managed to suppress the pain. Convinced myself I had dealt with it all. Apparently, I had not. I haven't cried in what seems like forever. The last response to my tears was to toughen up, and I haven't cried since. Didn't want to now, but I was overwhelmed by emotion and completely broke down. No time to even grab a drink. Reached the closest chair, and that was that. Would have lost it sooner had I not needed to concentrate on the road. Good thing I keep a box of tissues on the end table."

"Glad you made it home safely. How did you cope all these years?"

"My friend, Stacy, introduced me to marijuana, and we bonded quickly. Her family had moved in across the street from the pub. Stacy was in high school and I was in eighth grade. I was kind of a loner. Stacey must have felt sorry for me and befriended me. Guess she was taking me under her wing. She was my only friend at the time.

"Anyway, one Saturday Stacy invited me over. She had a group of friends over and brought me inside to introduce me. They were all just sitting around and I joined them. Someone lit up a joint and passed it around. Didn't say no, and I increased my number of friends. Liked that, but more importantly, I was enjoying a calm, floaty buzz.

"Started out strictly on the weekends. Nothing in excess, because catching a buzz was enough. By limiting my intake, my drug use flew under the radar, till sophomore year. Had my license then and hung out with friends the same age. We were partying every night and getting stoned. Marijuana released me from my insecurities, and I liked it. Skipped school more than I attended. This continued till the end of my sophomore year. During that summer, I threw myself into books. Reading became my drug of choice throughout the remainder of high school."

"Your grandfather must have been worried. I'm sure he hoped to provide a better life for you."

"I know my grandfather did, but he could not fix the damage that had been done. Especially since he was not the cause. I felt I'd found a way of dealing with my problems without troubling him, but obviously I didn't think through the whole skipping school idea. Didn't think about it at all, actually, just did it."

"So much for continuing to fly under the radar."

"That's for sure. My counselor called my grandfather, and he sat me down for a chat. He instructed me to clean up my act. Did not want to put restrictions on me, but felt he'd have no choice if I didn't do better. From that point forward, I attended all my classes, limiting myself to quick fixes, and made it through the remainder of the year physically in school but mentally craving my next high."

"That must have been hard. You did, after all, tell me about being done with school before you were done with school."

"Definitely no picnic, but better than the alternative of my grandfather grounding me. Could not have that, nor did I want to disappoint him. Little did I know my grandfather had made summer plans for me."

"What sort of plans? Book camp?"

"What?"

"You did say you threw yourself into books that summer."

"Ha ha. Good one, but not quite. My grandfather had me committed to rehab. And here I foolishly thought I'd played it cool. All the arrangements were made with the help of my counselor. The plan being for me to finish out the year with my admittance scheduled for the last day of school. My disappearance would be less conspicuous during the summer.

"Anyway, I can safely say I was in no condition for reading at that point, not with having to go through detox first. Once I could have visitors, my grandfather brought me the first Devlin Scott novel. I had to have something to do to pass the time. I was hooked from the beginning, and he continued to bring more of his books each visit. Found I actually enjoyed reading, losing myself in a good story. I'd been lost in worse places."

"Sounds like you found a hobby that helped you. When did you start writing?"

"As part of my therapy, I was given a journal. It was supposed to be used to chronicle my feelings. Did enough sharing in sessions, so fuck that shit. Reading Devlin's books inspired me to write. So, I used the journal to start the process and began writing short stories."

"How did that go over?"

"Not very well at first, to be honest with you. A private session had been scheduled with Jennifer, my assigned therapist, for the purpose of evaluating my journal. Jennifer was sitting behind her desk when I arrived. Handed over the journal and had a seat. Immediately saw her agitation while reading, and she promptly looked up at me to ask what this was. Told her I'd been writing short stories and was actually enjoying it.

"As a therapist, Jennifer couldn't very well stay upset. After all, I was doing something constructive. She calmed down, began reading again, and told me it was good. Even encouraged me to keep it up, and went so far as to say I might have a promising future. And was well on my way to being released. Got my discharge papers a week before school started.

"Due to truancy, I had to repeat tenth grade. That was a bummer, but I felt better than I had in a long time. Through writing, I found a purpose, allowing me to reinvent myself. Additionally, my newfound interest in reading improved my ability to focus. The spirited girl I'd once been in our neighborhood returned, without being drug-induced. I'd only drink socially, but not excessively. I had no need until recently, when you helped me. Enough talking and speaking of drinking, let's have a nightcap. I did not intend to rehash all this, and I apologize."

"No apology necessary, and I'll have my usual, but I do have one more question." We stepped out onto the veranda, and Kerrie began making our drinks at the wet bar. We liked to enjoy our drinks poolside.

"What is it, Columbo?"

"Cute. Nice to have you back. You mentioned our neighborhood. Are you up for a reunion? It's just your life sure went downhill after you moved away. Be honest."

"Geez, do you want me to feel bad?" I recognized Kerrie was joking with me, and we both had a good laugh. "The key word is after. I'm excited about revisiting the place where life was good, simple, not complicated. Now for that drink." Kerrie handed me my whiskey on the rocks as she sipped her rum.

"Great! I'll call Ashlyn to see if there has been a date set yet."

"Just let me know. I am really glad you came over, Erin. I'm feeling much better, which is surprising, because I always expected to feel worse after talking about it."

"Friends look out for each other. I wanted to help, and came over here with the intention of getting you to speak to me. Couldn't very well help unless you did." I slid off the barstool, "I should be getting home. Busy day tomorrow with my waterbed and pool table being delivered. You should come over."

"Have to work on my book, but I will definitely make a point to stop by. See ya."

"You better. See ya." Walking home, I could not help but feel pleased with the outcome. Of course, there was more to Kerrie's story, as she had indicated, but I never expected to find out everything in one afternoon and was satisfied I got her speaking at all. Mission accomplished.

12

UPDATE

As soon as I got home, the search began for my cellphone so I could check for missed calls. I was always putting it down in different places. It would have been helpful to have a clicker to locate phones. Well, it would have been, if I were also diligent about putting the clicker back in the same place.

My thoughts went to calling Kirk to give him an update, then calling Ashlyn to get an update. My thoughts ended up acting as a reminder. Since Kirk was the last person I spoke to, the memory clued me in on where I'd left the cellphone. There were many missed calls. Most of them were from Kirk, but the last one was from Ashlyn.

It never ceased to amaze me how Ashlyn would happen to call right after I'd mentioned her, like tonight. Sometimes I just thought about her and she called. She said the same about me. We'd remained close friends throughout the years, which explained our strong connection. I sometimes wondered if it was a fluke or if it was possible our connection had given us an extra sense about each other.

I listened to my messages and hit call back on Kirk's voicemail. Kirk picked up pretty darn close to the first ring and was speaking rapidly and frantically. "Hey Erin. Is Kerrie okay?"

"Yes, she's fine. Take a breather."

"Sorry. It's just I called you several times and got worried something happened."

"I had left my phone at home. I was so focused on Kerrie I didn't think to bring it with me. Got home a few minutes ago and retrieved my phone. We had been talking all that time."

"So, did it have to do with the mother and daughter?"

"That was it. Kerrie has successfully bottled up her emotions for years, but the scene triggered a reaction that was too strong to suppress this time. She had to race out before she totally lost it. Saved that for the privacy of her own home. I found Kerrie buried in tissues. She had so many bunched in each hand it looked like her palms were producing them. Kerrie was crying hysterically, which was a long overdue cathartic release. Finally, she calmed down enough to open up. All problems from her past."

"It was good you were there, Erin, giving Kerrie a chance to talk them out. Much better for her than bottling the emotions up again."

"Agreed. Kerrie was getting back to herself before I left."

"Glad to hear it. That's all I need to know, so I'll let you go. And thanks, Erin."

"Oh, Kirk. There is something else I should let you know."

"What is it? Should I be concerned?"

"Not at all. You talked in our earlier conversation about our being from the same hometown. I'll start by telling you all these problems started after she moved away. Anyway, my friend Ashlyn is planning a neighborhood reunion, and Kerrie and I are going. I think it will be good for her. One of the children from our street ended up buying the house Kerrie grew up in, and this is where the reunion is going to be held."

"Probably will be good for her. You did speak of happy childhood memories. When is the reunion?"

"Not sure yet. I plan on calling Ashlyn when we hang up to see if a date has been set."

"Okay. You can use my plane if you'd like. By the way, where are you all from? Kerrie never did say."

"That would be great. We're from a small town in Wyoming hardly anyone's heard of, which is probably why she didn't mention it. Anyway, I remember there was a mountain in walking distance and we got plenty of snow. It was actually a big grassy hill. Called it a mountain, because we loved to ski down it."

"Does Kerrie ski?"

"Yeah. She's a fantastic skier. Kerrie started at the age of three. She was so little, but took to it like a fish to water. By the time Kerrie was six, she put us older kids to shame."

"Ha. I'll have to make a note of that. Wait, I thought you didn't hang out together?"

"I didn't hang out with Kerrie, but that doesn't mean I never saw her. All our different age groups hung out in the same areas. We saw each other, but we were with our friends of the same age. The hill was the closest we all came to hanging out together. Kerrie was so adorable."

"I see. Must be what you meant by a close neighborhood. I will let my pilot know once you have a date."

"Yeah. Thanks, Kirk, and goodbye."

"Goodbye, Erin." I hung up my call with Kirk and immediately called Ashlyn.

"Hey, Erin."

"Hi, Ashlyn. Sorry I missed your call. I was over Kerrie's and left my phone at home."

"Everything all right?"

"Everything is fine. Mentioned to Kerrie I would call you to see if there was a date yet. Came home and found you had called me. How uncanny is that?"

"Really, but that happens to us a lot."

"I know. So, do you have a date?"

"I do, actually. Everyone is on board for a week from this Saturday. Will that work for you two, or is it too soon?"

"Works for me. The sooner the better. I know Kerrie is working on her new book, but she can write from anywhere. I'll check with her tomorrow."

"Are you telling me the truth about everything being fine?"

"Yes. Why?" After I asked, the answer immediately came to me. "Oh, because I said the sooner the better. Just meant I have been really looking forward to getting back and seeing everybody again. It's been too long."

"Oh, and I agree. The response has been amazing."

"I spoke with Kirk, my director friend, prior to calling you back. I informed him of the reunion and our plans to attend, and he offered his plane."

"I remember you telling me about him. Did not know he had his own plane, though."

"Yes, the plane is for his production company. Kirk has several preferred locations he enjoys shooting his films in."

"Must be nice. Okay, get back to me about Kerrie. Talk to you soon."

"I will. Goodbye, Ashlyn." The day's end had been extremely busy, and the next day was going to start out that way. I decided to turn in so I would be fully rested.

13

_____

BRAINSTORMING

Got up in the morning feeling refreshed. I believed I was finally ready to start the writing process on my new book. Taking some time away had helped to clear my head. All the clutter had been clogging up my thinking, causing me to stay blocked. My brain needed to become a clean slate to allow new ideas to enter. I had several notions floating around and thought it best to jot them down before they were forgotten. But not before I had gotten my first cup of coffee.

While the coffee brewed, I grabbed a bowl, reached for a box of cereal, and took them to the table. I returned to pour a cup of coffee and pulled a carton of milk from the fridge. As I sat there preparing my breakfast, my mind wandered from one thought to another.

First, I reviewed yesterday's events. Specifically, how much better I felt after revealing some of my past to Erin. Obviously, it had been long overdue, considering I was on overload in my attempts to remain private. Guess the floodgates were bound to open up sometime.

Next, I remembered shopping for cereal as a kid. This memory came from reading the cereal box as I scooped some marshmallow charms onto my spoon. The thought was briefly interrupted by my questioning why I felt the need to grip the side of the box when reading. As if it would somehow move and I would lose my place. Whatever, back to my shopping. As a kid I based my decision not on flavor but on which cereal box had the best prize. I'd get home, immediately open the box, and reach my arm all the way to the bottom in search of the treasure.

When the prize was successfully in my grasp, my arm made its way back to the surface, bunching up the cereal as it went. By now the box had taken on a slightly different shape, bulging at the seams. I imagined the top might have been a bit challenging to close after that, but I couldn't recall any major issues. After all, I had gotten my prize. The end justified the means.

Childhood memories led me to the upcoming reunion, and I made a mental note to myself to check with Erin later for a possible date. I looked down at my bowl and found it empty, which matched my coffee cup. Time to kick it into gear.

I found my laptop on the coffee table and headed outside. I set up at the table and created an outline, including my premise and some key points I wanted to target. The goal, naturally, was to create scenes that addressed the points, therefore making them concepts for plot. A flow would be generated, hopefully, giving birth to each chapter, taking on a life of its own and unfolding a story at my fingertips. This was writing at its best and in its purest form, when creativity was unleashed and ideas popped into my head quicker than I could type.

Focusing on the first point, I began typing, my fingers racing across the keyboard. The words of Devlin came to me about needing to relax to allow the creative flow to take hold. Well, those words were ringing true today, and the writing process was able to begin.

Several chapters in, my pace was beginning to slow down. Probably a sign of a good place to stop. I turned around and looked at my pool. Looked so inviting. Pleased with the day's accomplishments, I raced inside to change into my bathing suit and quickly returned.

I eased down the steps until my feet hit the bottom of the pool. Spotted the waterfall and swam toward it. I surfaced on the far side of the waterfall and contentedly sat in my grotto. Loved seeing all the colorful plants.

Antonio, Erin's ex-groundskeeper, definitely had a green thumb. I was very pleased with his work. I watched as he worked to add more plants to the landscape, and I swam over to get a closer look. Sitting on the edge of the pool, I continued to watch. Antonio caught me looking in his direction. "Is there a problem, Miss? I mean, Kerrie. Am I doing something you don't like?" Antonio asked, conscientiously. He was about medium height with a medium build.

"Relax. I was just admiring your work. You are a true artist, Antonio."

"I am glad you think so, and I want to thank you for hiring me."

"No need to ever thank me. I'm just grateful you accepted the position."

"Well, it is important to me you know I appreciated the offer."

"I do know. I can see your appreciation through your attention to detail in maintaining the landscape and through your passion for designing an attractive garden. And the pool is sparkling. Can I get you a drink or something to eat, perhaps?"

"I am okay, Miss. Kerrie. My wife packed me a lunch. Do you mind if I call you Miss Kerrie? I'm having trouble remembering to call you by your first name."

"That will be fine. I was lucky enough to have a sample of your wife's cooking over at Erin's one time. Believe she was dropping off your lunch and made extra for Erin. I would be okay with her packing me a lunch, as well. Just kidding, but I am very envious of the family she works for. I would hire her in a heartbeat if it doesn't work out for some reason. Maria, right?"

"Yes. We have a little girl, Nicky, who is four years old."

"I remember. Nicky was with Maria that day. She is adorable. You make a good looking family."

"Thank you."

"It's awfully hot out here. At least let me get you something to drink. I made some iced tea, my grandfather's recipe."

"Okay then. Does sound refreshing."

"Great! Be right back." Actually sounded good to me, also. I went inside, took down two glasses from the cabinet, dispensed some ice from the door of the refrigerator, and poured in the tea. Then I returned to Antonio and handed him a glass, from which he took a sip.

"Thanks, Miss Kerrie. This is tasty and refreshing."

"You're welcome, Antonio, and I'm glad you like it." I caught a glimpse of Erin standing on her veranda with her arms folded and foot tapping.

"Don't tell me you forgot about dropping by," Erin hollered.

"Okay, I didn't. Was everything delivered? Planned on coming over after your furniture arrived."

"I don't believe you, but everything is here. Come over and check it out."

"Let me just cover up and I'll be over." Antonio handed me his glass.

"That hit the spot. I'll be getting back to work now."

"Okay. I will be next door. Forgot all about dropping by. Oh well. Be sure and help yourself to more tea. The pitcher is in the refrigerator, and I'll leave your glass beside it."

"Miss Kerrie, were you serious about what you said earlier? You know, about the family Maria works for."

"Absolutely. I am envious of them."

"No, about if things did not work out."

"Oh! You mean hiring her in a heartbeat. The answer is yes. Why?"

"I hesitate to say. After all, you have been more than generous to me. It's just the family is moving. Job transfer. They would love it if Maria would go with them, but we are settled here."

"Don't say another word. It's a done deal. That is, if she is willing to work for me. Talk to Maria about it once you get home and let me know."

"The thing is, Maria has a lot of pride. Probably would not be too happy with me if she knew I told you. I know Maria planned on stopping by here today after work. Like she usually does."

"I see. I'll look out for her. Erin and I are going to be hanging out around her pool house. Don't worry. I will be discreet when speaking with her. Maria won't suspect you said anything. Well, better be getting over there."

"Appreciate it, Miss Kerrie." Antonio then walked over to the garden to finish his planting. I brought the glasses inside, placed Antonio's beside the pitcher and mine in the sink, raced to my bedroom to cover up, and then raced next door. Erin was lounging, as Davide tended to her pool. So focused on him, she did not hear me come up alongside her.

"Okay Erin, I'm here." Erin jumped at the sound of my voice and quickly looked at me.

"Well, it's about time!" Davide looked up and smiled at us. He was so good-looking.

"Does not appear you were suffering waiting for me. And you know what I mean." Erin smiled big.

"How is Antonio doing?"

"Love Antonio. He certainly adores his wife and little girl. We talked about them today. This actually turned out better for both of us. I believe sometimes things just have a way of working out the way they're supposed to. The plans we have are not necessarily what is meant to be."

"I totally agree, Kerrie. Shall we check out the pool house?"

"Yes. Has Davide seen your purchases yet?" Erin stood up, and I followed her to the pool house.

"Not yet. He arrived not long before you came over and bee-lined it to the pool." We stepped inside, and I was amazed. The waterbed looked awesome, all made up with masculine bedding. The pool table situated beside the wet bar typified classy. I peeked behind the wet bar and found everything expertly stocked, as I had suspected.

"Erin, you really could be an interior decorator. Definitely have a knack for it. Just sayin'. The whole décor is very stylish. I like the royal blue cloth in the pool table. Good choice. It's a refreshing change from the usual green color I'm used to seeing."

Erin led me to the linen closet. "Open it up." I did as I was told and saw shelves of neatly folded and sorted washcloths, hand towels, and bath towels. "I credit you for this."

"Nicely done. I have no doubt you would have thought of it eventually. It was at the forefront of my mind only because at hotels I dread running out of towels. Especially at the beach with all the sand."

"Me too. Oh, and I spoke with Ashlyn. Let's go back outside, and I will tell you all about it."

"Okay, but help me be on the lookout for Maria."

"Why?"

"I am going to hire her. Never mind. I'll explain it later. Is there a date yet?"

"Okay. And yes, Ashlyn said everyone is on board for a week from this Saturday. Hope that works for you, because I know you're working on the book."

"Yeah, but I can write from anywhere. My agent is pretty flexible."

"Told Ashlyn I thought you could, but would check." I spotted Maria walking toward Antonio.

"Hey, there's Maria. Do you mind if I invite her over?"

"Not at all."

"Hey Maria!" I shouted, managing to get her attention, and waved her over.

"Hello, Kerrie and Erin. Nice to see you both. How can I help you?"

"First, have a seat. Haven't had an opportunity to talk to you, and with Antonio working for me now, I felt it was time for us to finally speak. Do you have time to chat with me a bit?"

"Yes, I would like that very much. I've often wanted to talk, but you were always busy, and I didn't want to disturb you."

"Aww, you're too sweet. I would have loved and welcomed the interruption, so do not ever feel that way. I can always use a break. Anyway, do you remember the day I was over here and you brought extra food?"

"Yes, I do."

"It was delicious. Remembering what a good cook you are, I told Antonio I would not mind if you packed me a lunch as well. Also told him I am envious of the family you work for. He just smiled, but I mean it. They are very lucky to have you."

"I appreciate your kindness, Kerrie. The family you speak of is moving. They would have kept me employed if I'd been willing to move with them, but this is my home. They figured as much, but needed to make sure. Said I'd become part of their family, and will miss me."

"I'm sorry, Maria, and am even sorry for them. I can see how you all could be so close. Have you made other arrangements for work?"

"Not as yet."

"I don't know what offers you've received, but I would love for you to consider working for me. Think about it and get back to me." Maria began to cry. "I did not mean to upset you."

"You haven't. These are tears of joy. It's just I have been so worried. This is my last week of work, and I've had no offers. I've put on a brave face so Antonio would not see my concern. I need no time to think about it, Kerrie. If you are serious about hiring me, I accept." In my excitement, I leaped up and gave her a hug.

"I am so glad. You have made me very happy, Maria."

"I feel the same way. Do you mind if I go tell Antonio the news?"

"Not at all. We will have many opportunities to chat now." Maria broke into a beautiful smile. Erin and I watched as she made her way over to Antonio with some pep in her step. We continued watching as Maria told Antonio the news. Their conversation ended in a sweet embrace with Maria's back to me. During the hug, Antonio gave me the thumbs up.

"So, where did we leave off, Erin?"

"Kerrie, that was very smooth. I love the two of them, and hope they don't have any hard feelings toward me. Maria was pleasant enough, but do you think she just put that on for your sake?"

"Doubt it. It's not like you fired Antonio. I think of it more like a switch, and they understand the power of attraction. They are married, after all. And you and Davide make an attractive couple."

"Thanks for that, and yes, we do. Okay, back to the topic of the reunion."

"Right. A week from this Saturday, did you say?"

"Yeah. Does that work for you?"

"That's perfect. I was thinking about it this morning over a bowl of cereal. That's another story. Never mind. I am really looking forward to it, and will pack up my laptop for my writing."

"Great! I am excited too. Also, I told Kirk about it, and he offered his plane to get us there. Oh, and what is your book about, anyway?"

"Sweet! It's another crime mystery with the same detective."

"Awesome! Maybe another movie part for me. Are you writing a series?"

"I wouldn't mind if that were to happen. It will be a series in the sense I am using many of the same characters, but the books do not have to be read in order. Maybe the first one as an introduction to the characters, but I hope the following books can stand on their own. Different cases and totally different stories."

"Totally awesome! I am going to be busy."

"Hope so. I am going to head back now. Want to enjoy my pool some more before the sun goes down. See you later for our usual evening drink, unless you are otherwise occupied," I said, with a couple of winks.

"Should be done by then," Erin replied with some return winks. Antonio and Maria were long gone by the time I arrived home. I swam a bit and then climbed into the spa. Starting to feel sleepy, I got out and lay on a lounge chair. This was a good day, I thought to myself. Then slipped off to dreamland.

14

INTERRUPTED NAP

Woke up to a tapping on my foot. Opened my eyes to see Erin standing over me once again. "I am beginning to wonder if you ever sleep in your bed," she remarked.

"Well, I've long been wondering if you sleep at all. How is it you have so much energy? Please bottle some and give it here." Noticed her holding an empty glass. "Did you start without me?"

"Yes, I sleep. Don't know about my energy, just do. And I would never start without you. Wouldn't very well be our evening drink if I did, now would it?"

"Suppose not." Erin reached out her glass to me, and I got to bartending. Whiskey on the rocks for her and rum on the rocks for me, as usual. "Did Davide get your pool all taken care of?"

"All spotless. After Davide finished, I showed him the pool house."

"And? I know he couldn't help but like it. My question is did he thank you in the same way as before?"

"You know it." Erin was beaming ear to ear.

"I am truly happy for you, Erin." Lifted my glass and said, "Here, here!"

"Appreciate it, Kerrie. You do know I am secretly rooting for you and Kirk to get back together."

"Not too secretly, since you just told me. We've agreed to be friends and see where it leads. Who knows? Maybe we will, but for now we're taking it slow."

"It was only an expression, and happy to hear it. Anyway, I also wanted to tell you I'm glad you called Maria over to my house, rather than handling it privately. I enjoyed witnessing such a touching moment."

"I'm glad, and that reminds me of a fleeting thought I had earlier. You don't think Maria realized I already knew, do you? Wouldn't want Antonio catching any grief."

"Not at all. Having her join us was a good idea. Made it seem like a girl chat."

"That's why I handled it that way. Thought speaking with her privately might be suspicious, I hope you're right."

"I am. Like I said, very smooth. Patio furniture is coming tomorrow, so I'm going to call it a night. Bye Ker."

"Nice to hear my nickname again. Bye, and love ya girlfran."

"With everything going on lately, guess I fell out of the habit. Love ya too."

"Guess I did, too. Bye Rin." I was by now wide-awake and thought about calling Kirk. Picked up my cellphone off the bar and saw he was calling me. "Hey, Kirk, crazy timing. I just picked up my phone to call you."

"Maybe crazy timing has nothing to do with it. I'm actually outside your door. Are you up for company?"

"Absolutely. Come on in, I'm out back." Soon Kirk was standing in the doorway. "Can I get you a drink?"

"Sure." Kirk sat down on a barstool. "I'll have what you're having." I was sitting in my usual spot behind the bar. Since I was serving, there was no point in moving. "I have to say you scared the hell out of me." As Kirk was speaking, I dropped cubes into a glass and poured out the rum. Freshened my glass, too, while I was at it. "Did not know what happened." I slid his drink in front of him, and Kirk took a sip. "Hope you're not mad I called Erin."

"That was fine. Erin being here with me helped. I always found it easier to keep my past private. I gather the emotions have built up over time and became more than I could bear." I took a sip before I continued. "As far as scaring the hell out of you, I seem to be doing that a lot lately." Kirk wore an empty expression. "Joking, Kirk. I'm honestly not poking fun."

"I didn't think you were. Are you better now?"

"Just wanted to make sure. I am. Sorry about taking off on you, but I had to get out of there."

"I understand. Erin explained the urgency."

"Did she explain anything else?"

"No, that was all. Just explained why you were in such a hurry to leave. I only needed to know you were all right and nothing more." I noticed our glasses were empty and served another round.

"Appreciate that, Kirk."

"Of course, if you ever need to talk, I am here for you as well. If not, that's fine, too. I also understand you and Erin are visiting your hometown. The fact you and Erin reconnected after all these years makes for a great story."

"Spoken like a true director. Always in search of a good storyline. Erin mentioned you offered your plane."

"That is correct."

"Extremely generous of you." Kirk was looking mighty hot this evening. Thought I remembered seeing him wearing his swimsuit and glanced over the bar to confirm.

"Glad to do it. And were you checking me out? You were, weren't you?"

"No, confirming my recollection of you having your swimsuit on. Would you care to take a swim? Antonio has the pool sparkling."

"Sounds nice! Do I need to be jealous of Antonio?"

"You know Antonio is my lawn guy or groundskeeper, whatever you prefer to say. He is also a happily married man with the most adorable little girl, Nicky. I hired his wife, Maria, this afternoon. She is a fabulous cook. I've been in need of a housekeeper and got lucky.

"The family she previously worked for got a job transfer. They wanted Maria to move with them, but naturally, her home is here. Their loss is definitely my gain." I walked around the front of the bar and noticed Kirk eyeing me intently. Ignoring him, I moved toward the pool, knowing he would not be far behind.

"I'm happy for you. Now you have a full staff. I must say you are looking mighty hot this evening." I was always amazed by how we shared the same thoughts.

"I was thinking the same exact thing about you."

"Really? Good to know." We swam around for a bit, but I made a point to keep a good distance between us. He was looking good, and alcohol only intensified my hormones. It did absolutely nothing to strengthen my resistance. With constant thoughts of fucking Kirk inhabiting my brain, I stopped under the waterfall to cool off, and then slowly approached the spa. I climbed in and sat down. Kirk soon joined me. I pointed to the opposite side for him to sit.

"Sit there, and I'll be right back. Getting a refill. Can I get yours while I'm up?" Having the drink would keep my hands busy.

"No, thank you. I'm good."

"Okay then. Suit yourself." I topped off my glass, returned to the spa, and reclaimed my spot across from Kirk. Took a sip and rested my arms on the pavement, mindful of Kirk's every move. Kirk looked confused.

"Why are we sitting opposite each other?"

"Well, in staying true to our agreement of taking it slow, this seating arrangement is necessary. It's safer for us to keep a distance, and that's all there is to it."

"I see. Safer for whom, exactly? Just curious."

"Don't care to share that with you."

"That's okay. You just did. No worries. I will sit here like a good scout and continue talking. When you finish your drink, I will make my exit."

"Another directorism. This has been nice, Kirk, and I'm glad you stopped by."

"Am glad you're glad. Feel free to stop by my place any time." I felt myself immediately tense up, which must have reflected on my face. "Too soon?"

"Too soon, but it's great having my friend back. I have missed our long conversations." My next sip was regrettably my last.

"Me too, and it appears you have finished, so I will depart."

"Let me get you a towel." We exited the spa, and I grabbed us a couple towels from the supply cabinet. I temporarily placed my glass in their place on the shelf.

"Do you mind if I borrow it for my car? I'll walk around to the front."

"Sure, that will be fine. You're welcome to walk through the house, if you'd like."

"Let's just say, it would be safer for me not to. Can I at least get a goodbye kiss?"

"I understand, and no. Time for you to go." I made a shooing motion with my hands and watched as he rounded the side of the house. Turned around, picked up my glass, and returned it to the bar, when I spotted Kirk's sunglasses. Hadn't noticed him laying them down or even having them, for that matter. Snatched them up and ran after him. "Kirk! Kirk!" I yelled, hoping he'd hear me. Luckily, he did. Kirk was leaning against his car when I reached him. "You left your sunglasses."

"Oh!" I stretched out my arm to hand the sunglasses to him. Kirk's fingers brushed against my hand when he retrieved them. That simple touch gave me goose bumps, and I stepped back. "Are you okay?" asked Kirk. The feeling of his flesh making contact with mine had set off my reaction.

"Yes. No. Yeah, I'm fine." I was struggling with an inner battle.

"Which is it?"

"Fuck it!" I said out loud, and stepped closer to lean in for a brief kiss. I backed off and walked to the front door. Leaning against it, I saw Kirk advancing toward me.

"What was that?"

"Your goodbye kiss. Was it all right?" Kirk stopped right in front of me.

"I'm not sure. Think you might need to kiss me again." I leaned in again, and Kirk placed his hands on my hips, pulling me toward him. Felt his hand resting on my breast as we continued to kiss. I pulled back and we looked into each other's eyes.

"Better?" I asked

"Much, but could always be better," Kirk replied. I reached one hand back to open the door and with the other pulled him inside. Reaching the bedroom, Kirk handed me the towel, which I took in the bathroom and dropped on the floor along with my bikini. I stepped outside the bathroom and faced Kirk. He was turning down the sheets in a rush.

"What about now? Is this better?" I gradually made my way back to Kirk. He looked up and quickly shed his clothes in response.

"Definitely getting there." Once at arm's length, Kirk lifted me up and scooted me onto the bed. My hands reflexively grabbed his hips as I felt him slide inside me.

Our bodies were locked in and hips fully engaged, solidifying our yearning and fulfilling our need. Kirk rolled over onto his back and pressed up against my side. "I believe we got there." We turned on our sides and faced each other, both grinning in satisfaction.

15

MAKING ARRANGEMENTS

My alarm clock buzzed, starting my day in a state of confusion. My eyes sprang open to the blasting in my eardrum, and it took me a minute to identify the sound. I wasn't confused because I'd been in a deep sleep but because I never set my alarm. After rolling over to hit the off button, I rolled onto my other side to hopefully get a few more minutes of shut eye, and saw my robe neatly laid out with a note attached to it.

Kerrie,

Get your ass up, put this on, and come out to breakfast.

Thanks,

Kirk

I followed the instructions on the note, with the exception of brushing my teeth before heading out to the kitchen. I walked up behind Kirk, wrapped my arms around him, and peeked over his shoulder to watch as he whisked some batter. "Good morning, sleepy head," Kirk said, and followed with a peck on my cheek.

"Morning, Kirk. You set my alarm, didn't you?"

"Yes, I did. Can't have you sleeping this beautiful day away. Now sit down, and breakfast will be ready in a minute. Oh, and grab some coffee first. I would have poured you a cup already but didn't want it getting cold."

"That's fine." I got the coffee, took my seat in front of a previously set spot, and waited. Kirk poured his mixture into a waffle iron and set the timer.

In the meantime, Kirk sliced some strawberries and bananas. The timer went off, and he used a fork to carefully remove the waffle and put it on a plate. He sprinkled some flour and topped it with his sliced fruit. Opening the refrigerator, he pulled out whipped cream and returned to the waffle, spraying some on top. He brought the plate over and, grabbing a pitcher of orange juice, poured some in the glass sitting beside me. Lastly, he added butter and syrup to the table. "Eat up." Kirk sat down next to me.

"You have certainly been a busy bee this morning." I fixed the waffle and, taking a bite, got whipped cream above my lip. Picked up a napkin to wipe it off. "Aren't you having one?"

"Wait, I'll get that." Kirk leaned into me and licked the whipped cream off. "Got it," Kirk said, with a silly grin. "No. Need to take off after I clean up the kitchen. What do you mean about me being busy?"

"What do I mean? Well, for starters, you set an alarm I never use. In addition, I did not have any of the ingredients used to make this wonderful breakfast. Did not even have the waffle iron."

"Oh, that. I went to the store and picked up a few items. Was that okay?"

"Absolutely! This is delicious." I faintly heard my sliding door open.

"Kerrie," Erin called out.

"In the kitchen, Erin." She soon appeared in the doorway. Staring at Kirk and me, a broad smile came over her face.

"So Kirk, did you come over to make Kerrie breakfast, or did we have a sleepover?" Kirk's face cracked into a broad smile, too. Erin rapidly clapped her hands together several times in excitement. "This makes me so happy!" Erin raced up behind us, wrapped her arms around our necks, and kissed our cheeks. "That taking it slow plan was fucking bullshit!"

"Can I fix you a waffle, Erin?" asked Kirk. "Be a shame for the extra batter to go to waste."

"Sure. If you put it that way, I'd be glad to help." Kirk got up and moved to the counter. "Oh, and Kirk, the reunion is a week from tomorrow."

"Okay. I'll let my pilot know." The timer went off, and Kirk repeated the process. Erin poured a cup of coffee, and Kirk handed her the plate.

"Thank you, Kirk." Erin came back over and took Kirk's seat. She cut the waffle up and took a bite.

"Don't mention it." The cleanup went quickly.

"We have Kirk's plane, but do you have any ideas of where to stay?" I asked. Kirk walked over and placed his hands on my shoulders.

"A few. Would you mind if I went ahead and made all the arrangements? I know planning stresses you out."

"Yes, it does. So that's perfectly fine with me."

"Hate to interrupt, but I'm going to head out. Enjoy your day ladies."

"Okay, Kirk. Thanks again for breakfast." Kirk released his grip.

"Happy to do it." Facing me, he spoke once more. "And Kerrie, keep the whipped cream and fruit. Might come in handy at a later time."

"If that's the case, you might need to pick up some chocolate syrup and cherries."

"I can do that. See ya." I could tell by the expression on Erin's face that our banter entertained her.

"Goodbye, Kirk," I responded, with emphasis.

"You go girl," said Erin. She finished the last few bites of waffle and picked up her plate.

"Leave it, Rin. I'll get it in a minute." Kirk was gone, so it was safe to pull out her nickname.

"Best be leaving, too. My patio furniture is being delivered this afternoon."

"Okay. I'll check it out later this afternoon. I plan on taking a dip in my pool and then getting started writing again."

Erin stood up and said, "See ya later, Ker."

"Bye, Rin." I cleared the table and loaded the dishwasher. There wasn't much clean up left, thanks to Kirk. I entered the family room and noticed my laptop located in its usual spot on the coffee table, perfectly positioned in front of the sofa. Kirk must have returned the laptop to its rightful place, because I, for obvious reasons, had forgotten all about it.

Plopping onto the sofa, I picked up the laptop. In an attempt to jog more ideas, I reviewed my notes and read the chapters from yesterday. Different scene possibilities were generating in my mind, and I added them to the notes. The time on the laptop alerted me that an hour had passed. This start would be a good place to work from after my swim, but first I had to shower.

I hit the shower, enjoying the warm water running down my body. I closed my eyes while rinsing the shampoo, and then turned around. Keeping my eyes closed, I lifted my face to the showerhead and rinsed off some more. Suddenly, I felt hands rubbing my behind and moving around to between my thighs. "Showering without me, babe?"

In a breathy voice I answered, "You had left, Kirk." Gently and methodically lathering his way up my body, he began fondling my breasts, his fingertips tickling my nipples.

"I'm back now." Kirk's mouth started moving slowly from the base of my neck toward my earlobe. I was held captive by the sensation. Kirk turned me around, held my face, and pulled me in for a long, sensuous kiss. The kiss led to his sliding down my body and lifting me up with my legs wrapped around him, and working our way to a release of mutual satisfaction.

I stepped back under the showerhead to rinse off my recently lathered body and switched places with Kirk so he could do the same. I got out, wrapped a bath towel around me, and dried my hair with a hand towel. Kirk stepped out, grabbed a bath towel to dry his hair, and wrapped it around his waist. "I thought you were gone for the day," I said.

"Me too, but I had to bring back the chocolate syrup and cherries you requested."

"I see."

"What's on tap for today?"

"My plan is to take a swim and get back to writing. I was working on it earlier, collecting new ideas. I have a pretty good place to start from after my swim."

"Sounds like a good plan." I finished drying off, dropped the towel on the floor, and aimed for the walk-in closet. I picked out a bikini and got dressed. When I came out, I noticed Kirk had on a different shirt and swimsuit.

"Did you go home and change?"

"No, babe. Told you I picked up your items. Figured I could always use more swim trunks and shirts."

"Did you really get the syrup and cherries?"

"Of course I did. If you're going to make a statement like that, I'm sure going to act on it." I didn't know whether he was pulling my leg or not. Withholding comment, I scooted out to the kitchen to check. I opened the refrigerator, and there they were, staring me in the face. I turned around just as Kirk was entering. "What? You didn't believe me, babe. Now that hurts."

"Yeah, right." I headed out to the family room and saw a bulging bag on the chaise chair. Curiosity got the best of me. I pulled out a skimpy red bikini and held it up. "Tell me, Kirk, did you try this on?"

"Oh yeah! Did I forget to mention buying you a swimsuit, also? Saw it and had to get it. Do you not like it?"

"Actually, I love that you bought it for me." We exited the family room for our swim. I noticed as I stepped out that the wet bar had been cleaned off. I knew I hadn't done it. I had started to before I spotted Kirk's sunglasses, and then had become otherwise occupied. I hadn't given it another thought, to tell you the truth.

Entered the pool and floated on my back until I reached the waterfall. Flipped over and swam through it to the grotto. Sat down on the rock ledge behind the waterfall. This time I let Kirk sit next to me. "I like sitting here. Find it calming."

"See what you mean. What is your new book about? I assume it'll be another crime novel. Hope you're using the same main characters."

"I am. Seems smart to stick with a formula that works. The characters are the formula. If they're relatable, likable, or have a redeeming characteristic to the reader, there lies the hook that pulls them deeper and deeper into the story."

"You're absolutely correct. I will tell you from a director's standpoint, strong characters are essential. From them, many stories can be made. Each plot, which in your case would be a different crime, allows for a whole new story that can stand alone."

"Wow! I said something very similar to Erin."

"Really?"

"Yes. She asked if I was writing a series. Told her only in the sense I was using many of the same characters. Apart from the first book to get to know the characters, I hoped the following books could stand on their own. Different cases and totally different stories."

"I'm not surprised. You know what they say about great minds thinking alike."

"Yes, I love that expression. Erin also expressed enthusiasm at the prospect of reprising her role."

"Don't see why not. *Misguided* was a mega hit and expanded Erin's popularity beyond music. Keep writing books like that, and we will become a force to be reckoned with."

"I like the sound of that."

"Stick with me, and we will make it happen."

"Guess I'd better get back to it, then."

"You do that, and I'm going to continue to hang out in the pool." I got out, dried off, and retrieved my laptop. Setting up at the table again, I looked over my scene ideas. Took the first one and worked to create a chapter around it. It was slow-going at first, but then I hit a groove, and created several more chapters. Rolled with it until I stalled. Twisted in my chair and saw Kirk looking my way.

I hadn't even realized Kirk was lying in the lounge chair behind me. He must have been quietly watching me work. "How long have you been watching me?"

"For a while. I enjoyed watching you work." I walked over to Kirk, straddled his legs, rested my hands on his chest, and gave him a kiss.

"What else do you enjoy?"

"I enjoyed that." Kirk pressed his mouth between my breasts and kissed. "And enjoy this." His mouth moved up my neck. I was catching the theme and received a flash of memory.

"Oh shit! Forgot about Erin. Told her I would check out her patio furniture."

"You certainly know how to kill a mood." Quickly got up and faced Erin's. I was relieved to see the furniture was just being delivered, and Davide was working in the yard.

"Come with me. I want you to meet Davide."

"Okay." Kirk got up, held my hand, and we started walking over. "I am glad he got the address wrong."

"Too funny. You heard about that?"

"Erin told me, which explained how you came to hire Antonio."

"Correct. Definitely a win-win." I wondered how much of the story Kirk knew. I stopped abruptly, released his hand, and we faced each other. "Hey Kirk, do you happen to know how I came to need a new lawn guy?"

"No. Is that a funny story, as well?"

"Depends on your perspective."

"Do you want to tell me?"

"Not particularly, but in the spirit of full disclosure, I probably should."

"Okay. Tell me."

"I was at a low point after our breakup. Dillon, my previous lawn guy, noticed me being out of sorts, not my usual enthusiastic self. Dillon felt bad for me, and as he asked what was wrong, put his arm around my shoulders. We both got caught up, Dillon with his desire to help me, and me with my desire to be helped." Erin's yell interrupted my explanation.

"You coming over or not?"

"Just a minute."

"Okay. Hurry up." I never looked away from Kirk when answering Erin.

"Anyway, Dillon became consumed with guilt because of his girlfriend, whom he adored. For me, it was a temporary interruption to my misery. We mutually decided to part ways. I called a household staffing agency, which had been recommended, and hired a replacement."

"Let me see if I have this straight. So, you slept with your previous lawn guy and hired a new lawn guy, who went to Erin's by mistake. She slept with your new lawn guy, and you hired her lawn guy. Does that about cover it?"

"Pretty much. The only part missing is that Davide is moving in to her pool house tomorrow. A crazy turn of events."

"That is funny."

"Told you it depended on your perspective. You're okay, then?"

"I can't very well be upset with you, considering the nature of our breakup. Did Erin or you ever tell Davide?"

"No. Nobody likes to hear about their mistakes, and we didn't see the point in possibly upsetting him. Besides, it all worked out for the best. Davide recently moved here from Italy, and Erin has an Italian heritage, which naturally comes with pride. She even has family living there."

"Sounds perfect." Kirk reached out to hold my hand, and we walked over to Erin.

"Is everything all right?" asked Erin. She was sitting on a wicker sofa with Davide.

"Yeah," I replied, "we just needed to finish our conversation. You two look cozy."

"We are. Nice to see you back, Kirk."

"Well, I had to drop off a few items."

"I bet. Kirk, this is Davide." Davide stood up and shook Kirk's hand.

"Nice to finally meet you, Kirk. Erin told me about how you first met."

"Seems ages ago now. I'm glad to meet you, too, Davide. Nice to put a face with a name."

"Yes, exactly." Davide turned to face me. "Hello, Kerrie. Erin tells me you're writing another book. Erin bought me your first book. To be honest, I'm not much of a reader, but your writing style hooked me from the beginning. All the twists and turns kept me guessing."

"Well, just don't stand there, take a seat," Erin said. Kirk and I sat down on the other sofa. There were two sofas, two chairs, and, of course, a canopy with the patio set." I looked to Davide to respond to his comments.

"Thank you, Davide. Glad you liked it."

"I did. Very much. Could I trouble you to sign my copy?" His request flattered me and instantly brought a smile to my face.

"I'd be happy to."

"Great, and thank you." Davide hopped up and raced into the pool house.

"Comfy furniture, Erin. Is tomorrow still move-in day?" I caught a glimpse of Davide racing back.

"It was going to be, but with only clothes to move, he's already moved in."

"Excellent!" Davide sat back down next to Erin and handed me the book.

As I was signing, Davide remarked, "The title can also describe the reader. Every time the book led my suspicions in one direction, new information that came to light sent me in another."

"True. Turns out the title can define many aspects, but I intended on it describing the lead detective. Have you seen the movie yet? Erin portrayed her perfectly."

"No. We plan on watching it together, and I can't wait to see her performance."

"So, Davide," Kirk jumped in, "is Erin treating you all right? The pool and yard look amazing."

"Yes, Erin has been most generous. We have much in common, and she is a lot of fun. And thank you, Kirk. I like to think of the yard as a beautiful painting I'm creating."

"Well, you have succeeded. Love all the colors."

"I try. Do you happen to shoot pool?"

"I have been known to play now and then. Why?"

"Would you be up for a match?"

"Sure." Davide got up and led the way.

"Let's all go in and have a drink at the wet bar," offered Erin. "This will be our evening drink, Kerrie."

"Works for me." We all had a great time, with plenty of laughter to go around. The evening ended with plans to get together again soon.

16

COUNTDOWN

I started the day early, wanting to get in a full day of writing or to write until I was empty, whichever came first. Back in my usual spot outside, I became so engrossed that I tuned out the world until my stomach made me aware of needing to eat. I checked the time at the bottom of the screen and saw it was already one. I realized I had been working for quite a while, and felt even hungrier.

A chicken salad sandwich sounded good to me. I always kept cans of chunk chicken breast on hand. The thought of the sandwich replaced my hopes of continuing to write.

I set off for the kitchen and started preparing my lunch. I had boiled some eggs earlier. Two of them had been my breakfast, and the rest were for snacking. I used my egg slicer and poured the slices into the mixture of chicken and mayonnaise. I only needed an onion, but remembered I didn't have one. A light bulb with Erin's name on it turned on. She was a much better shopper.

I raced over to Erin's and let myself in, which was what we usually did. I began yelling out her name until she responded. She came running to meet me with a frightened look. "Kerrie, what's wrong? Are you okay?"

"That depends on if you have an onion. Do you have one?"

"You came over here screaming because of an onion?"

"Yeah, I need one."

"I thought something was wrong."

"There is something wrong. I need a chicken salad sandwich, and in preparing the mixture, I needed to add an onion that I don't have." She shook her head, entered her kitchen, and returned with an onion.

"You seriously need help." I took the onion from her.

"Correction, I did need help." Before continuing, I held the onion at eye level. "But now you've helped. I can complete my mixture. Come over if you want to."

"Maybe I will. Does sound good." I raced back to fix my lunch. Chopped the onion and stirred in the bits along with some salt and pepper. Got a couple of slices of rye and made my sandwich. Took a bite to satisfy my worked-up taste buds and headed back to work with the rest, grabbing a bottle of water on the way out. I sat down beside my laptop and heard a ding sound, indicating I'd gotten an email. Clicked on my email to see the new message, and was excited to see it had come from Haley.

Ashlyn had told her about me attending the reunion, but she wanted to hear it from me. It had been years since we'd seen each other. Haley was a couple years older, and she had often palled around with Emily, who was her age. Emily was the sister of my friend Kate, whom I had spent a lot of time with, and who was my age. We had often been in close proximity of each other. Sometimes I had gone to Haley's house, and she had been cool about letting me hang out with her.

Both our families had season passes to Snow King Mountain. With Jackson Hole being so close, we spent many days together. Even stayed for the weekend on a few occasions.

Our moms would either hang back at the lodge chatting or head into town to check out the shops, so our dads would take us to Snow King Mountain. Ashlyn always hooked up with friends, leaving Haley and me to hang out together. And our dads, of course. We would alternate between skiing and tubing. Haley and I would hold on to each other's tubes and slide down the hill. She always had me giggling. I remembered her laugh being contagious.

I had started typing when Erin came up behind me. "Came over for lunch."

"Hey Rin. I just received an email from Haley. Sorry, go on in and help yourself. I put the salad in the refrigerator and left the rye on the counter."

"No apology necessary. I can see you're excited, and understandably so. It's been years since you two have made contact, and soon you'll be together again." Erin moseyed on in, and I got to typing. Our correspondence ended right before Erin came back out.

"Done responding already?" Erin placed her sandwich and drink down beside me. She repositioned a lounge chair and situated a little side table next to it.

"Yeah. Kept it brief since we'll have plenty of time to speak and catch up in a week. In fact, we closed with a plan to start a countdown and send an email each day with the number of days remaining."

"I love that." Erin finally got settled and had her first bite. "Yum, this is good. Definitely glad you came over for the onion."

"I know. Now you understand."

"Yeah, I can see the difference it makes. On another note, we have a place to stay, and it's a spacious suite."

"Sounds nice. May not have wanted to make any of the plans, but I'm going to pay my share."

"All taken care of. Just continue writing and keeping me in the movie business."

"I spoke with Kirk about your hopes to reprise your role. He didn't see any reason why not."

"Great! I'd hoped Kirk would say that. And relax about the room. I didn't pay for it, either. Kirk made all the arrangements. Once the plane lands, a limo will transport us to our hotel. I only paid for the champagne that will be waiting for us in the limo."

"Awesome! Didn't even think to ask this earlier, but when are we leaving, exactly?"

"Glad you asked, because I forgot to mention it. Thought about mentioning it at one point, but it quickly escaped my mind. We're arriving Thursday, allowing us a couple days to get settled and maybe go shopping or sightseeing."

"I love that idea. I'll put myself on "Do Not Disturb" status so I can make headway on my book. If I work on it while we're away, also, I should be close to finishing by the time we get back."

"Sounds like you have it all figured out. I will leave you to it then. I want to get back to Davide, anyway."

"I bet." Erin got up and began walking to the door with her plate and glass. "Here, give it to me. I have to go in anyway."

"Okay then. See ya Thursday, Ker."

"You know it."

17

TIME FLIES

The week flew by with my determination to make progress on the book. I managed to accomplish this goal by basically isolating myself from everyone. It was the only way to avoid interruptions or distractions. Thankfully, Kirk and Erin understood. They knew the nature of needing to stay focused and cooperated by respecting that need.

Another enormous help was Maria. She started on Monday, which made for perfect timing. I didn't have time to keep up with anything. Plates and glasses were stacked in the sink because I never unloaded the dishwasher, and hampers overflowed with backed up laundry. I was grateful Maria did not run straight out the door. She simply started quietly working her way through the chores.

I had never been the best housekeeper in the world, but I did pick up after myself. Well, eventually, anyway. The place looked immaculate. Maria even packed my bag. She told me to pick out what clothes I wanted to bring, and she would take care of the rest. Because all the laundry had been washed and neatly put away, I had plenty to choose from.

I rolled my luggage to the front door, with my pillow resting on top. Having my own pillow was a must. I always slept better with it. I was taking a mental inventory to make sure I hadn't forgotten anything, when I spotted Maria coming around the corner.

"Do you have everything, Kerrie? I packed the clothes and shoes you laid out, but didn't know about packing your toiletries."

"That's fine, Maria. I plan on buying those once we arrive." I had taken care of my personal items, but now I needed to check on my work items. "What about my laptop?"

"Behind you." I twisted around and saw the laptop case on the table beside the door. "I found it left on the coffee table. While packing the laptop up, I added your phone charger to the front pocket."

"Oh, right. Thank you, Maria. I would have forgotten that for sure. Well, I suppose that's everything. Can't imagine anything else, but if I have forgotten something, I'll just buy it there. I could not have gotten through this week without you."

"I am glad to be of help."

"You are more than a help, Maria. My stress level is greatly reduced having you here. There's too much to keep up with and meet a deadline, too, even if it is a self-imposed one. My agent is super flexible, but everybody runs out of patience at some point. I sent him everything I have to hopefully prevent that from happening."

"Anything special you need me to do while you're away?"

"No. Just keep doing what you're doing. And don't hesitate to call me about anything."

"Okay, Kerrie. Same to you. I'll say goodbye now and get back to work." I reached out to give Maria a hug before she busied herself. Gripping the luggage, I decided to wait for Wesley outside, and opened the door as Erin was entering.

"Where's your bag?" I asked.

"In the car."

"I'm confused. I thought Wesley was picking us up."

"He is." I looked over Erin's shoulder but didn't see him. "Wesley parked at my house. Kirk told him to, figuring I would have more luggage than you."

"Seriously? That's hilarious. Kirk knows you well."

"Yeah, real hilarious. As if the insinuation weren't bad enough, Kirk went on to tell Wesley he thought I might be packing the kitchen sink." Erin laughed as she told the story. She knew how she was. We always said it was good to be able to laugh at yourself, and made a point not to take ourselves too seriously because life could be too serious as it was.

"Ha, Wesley told you all this?"

"No, Kirk did."

"Kirk's here?" I didn't give Erin any time to answer. Swiftly placed the laptop on my shoulder and pillow under my arm, grabbed the handle of my luggage, and hurried over to Erin's. Kirk saw me, and we met halfway.

"Hey, babe."

"Hey, Kirk." He put his hand on the luggage, removed the laptop off my shoulder, and placed the strap onto his, but I kept my pillow. Erin moved up beside me. "Erin had me hysterical about your dialogue. Curious as to how you figured her for a packer."

"Can't say I knew for sure how Erin would be at packing, but let's just say after seeing all the purchases she made before Davide moved in, I figured it a safe bet she would not be a light one." We all had a good chuckle. Kirk approached Wesley, whose head was in the trunk. Wesley looked up at me. "Hey, Kerrie, I've missed you." Kirk put my bags in the trunk while Wesley and I talked.

"Missed you too, Wesley. Hear you two have been having fun joking around." A question mark seemed to appear on his face. "About Erin's packing," I added.

"Oh! Yeah. Her luggage is more weight than I lift at the gym."

"You can stop," Erin said through her laughter. Kirk high fived Wesley.

"Good one, Wesley," Kirk said. "Time to hit the road." Kirk opened one car door for me while Wesley opened the other for Erin. They both waited until we had buckled before closing the doors and getting in. Wesley started the car, and we were off.

"Are there any plans yet for when you arrive?"

Erin and I turned toward each other. Erin probably guessed from my expression I'd been too busy to think about it. "I hate to even say this, but we're thinking about maybe going shopping or sight-seeing," she said. I remembered she had mentioned that. "Shut up, Kirk."

"What? I didn't even say anything."

"Yeah, but I heard the wheels cranking in your head."

"I was about to say your plans sound like fun. Now, don't you feel bad?"

"Yeah, right. I seriously doubt it," remarked Erin.

"Just sayin'," said Kirk. "You are kind of quiet, Kerrie. Is everything okay?"

"Yes, I'm fine."

"Don't seem like it. Tell me what's on your mind."

"What's on my mind is my book. I've been working on it for days and I'm finding it hard to turn it off. No biggie."

"Are you pleased with your progress?"

"Yeah. It's just when you're focused on one thing for an extended period of time, it's hard to switch gears."

"I know what you're saying." Wesley put the car in park, popped the trunk, and got out. Kirk opened his door and said, "Be right back, babe." I looked out my window and saw the plane. Kirk and Wesley were talking with the pilot while workers loaded our luggage onto the plane. Kirk walked over to open my door, and Wesley raced around to open Erin's. Kirk put his hand out to help me. "We were waiting till the luggage was all in place," Kirk said. A curious wink followed his explanation. Despite my best effort I could not attach a meaning to the wink. Its suspiciousness could also have been the product of my overactive imagination, an occupational hazard.

I waved goodbye to Wesley as we passed each other. Erin and I boarded the plane while Kirk talked to the pilot. The interior was luxurious, with plush, gold leather seating. I picked a window seat and sank into it. The pilot entered the plane, Kirk right behind him. Kirk stood beside me. "Is everything to your liking?"

"Absolutely!"

"Excellent!" Kirk sat down, nodded to the pilot, and then turned to face me. "I hope you don't mind if I tag along to make sure the accommodations are satisfactory."

"Not at all. I didn't know you were joining us." The plane began taxiing to the runway.

"Only for a day, because I'm in final negotiations for my next project. I wouldn't mind doing some sightseeing."

"Great! I didn't know you were working on a new movie. Is it another book?" The plane began accelerating down the runway and, soon afterward, took off.

"No, it's an updated version of a classic thriller with a different plot twist."

"I'm sure it will be an instant hit."

"Counting on it. It's something I've been toying with for a while and is part of a greater project I'm working on. I don't have all the details figured out yet, but it has to do with classic thrillers."

"I'm sure it will be successful." I looked over at Erin, who looked sad.

"Do you think it's possible Erin is missing Davide, especially since you're here with me? Come to think of it, it's odd he wasn't around to see us off."

"I suppose." Kirk turned toward Erin. "Hey Erin, where was Davide this morning?"

"Don't know. Left early. Said he had something scheduled."

"And you don't know what?"

"No. I figured if Davide wanted me to know, he would tell me. I sure do miss him."

I leaned into Kirk and whispered, "I thought so. Maybe we should have let it be."

"I think I can help. I'm going to talk to her." Kirk unbuckled and stood next to Erin, placing his hand on her shoulder. He was talking low, so I couldn't hear him. Erin nodded, and he went through a doorway to the back. Erin unbuckled and joined me. I unbuckled, too.

"Kirk told me to sit next to you while he fixed us a drink."

"Great! What is it?"

"Two different special concoctions is all Kirk told me."

"Can't wait." Kirk soon appeared beside us holding only one drink, which he passed to me. He looked down at Erin.

"Didn't want you spilling the other drink in my seat, so I left it at yours. The cup holder will ensure it doesn't spill."

Erin and I looked at each other curiously. Why did Kirk think that she'd spill her drink? Seeking the answer, we abruptly stood up, and turned around to see Davide, the "cup holder", sitting in the seat next to Erin's. Erin let out a scream and almost knocked Kirk down. "And this is why I thought the drink would be spilled," he said. "See, I thought I might be able to help. You must be feeling better about Erin."

I walked over to Kirk teasingly and, feeling playful, said, "Let me demonstrate how much better I feel." I wrapped my fingers around his collar, pressed my body firmly against his, and planted an amorous kiss on his lips. After, I sat back in my seat to finish my drink.

"Love that demonstration, babe. I'm feeling pretty great myself."

"That was a sweet surprise, Kirk. When did you set it up?"

"I spoke with Davide about it while we were playing pool. I already knew I was going to tag along for a day, so I thought it only fair to include Davide. And I didn't want Erin feeling like a third wheel. Anyway, I had Davide come over early, and we dropped him off at the plane prior to picking you ladies up. I hated that Erin felt sad, but I also couldn't tell her. Would have spoiled the element of surprise." Kirk placed a finger to my lips, keeping me from responding, and touched his ear. We sat there quietly and heard some interesting sounds coming from the back.

"I think Erin is over her sadness. Sounds like it was well worth it," I said.

"I'll say. I believe they have just joined the mile-high club." I almost spit out my drink. A realization struck me.

"Aha! I've got it. You were referring to Davide with your comment about waiting till the luggage was all in place."

"You *did* catch my wink."

"Yes, but I dismissed it as my overactive imagination."

"I can see where that would be an occupational hazard."

"Do you have psychic vision to read my thoughts?" Kirk squinted questioningly. "Never mind. Forget I said anything."

"Okay. Consider it forgotten. I've been meaning to talk with you about something Erin mentioned to me. Made a mental note of it, even." I couldn't imagine what it was, but Kirk sounded awfully serious, which made me nervous.

"What is it?" I asked reluctantly.

"First, you never told me where you were from. Erin said it's a small town hardly anyone's heard of, which she believed to be the reason why. Is her explanation accurate?"

"It's true. I don't mind telling people I'm from Wyoming, if it could be left at that. But my answer always leads to the question of 'What part?' I answer and see a lost look, followed by the question of 'Where, exactly?' I then list the names of well-known cities nearby. I even tried cutting out a step by using Erin's line to qualify for an answer."

"How'd that work out for ya?"

"Didn't. My answer was always followed by the question of 'Which one?' Never understood their intent in knowing when I could guarantee they wouldn't have heard of it. It wasn't as if it held any special meaning, like it did for people from there. Anyway, found it easier to not offer the information in order to avoid the question coming back at me."

"That's fair. Next, Erin told me you're a fantastic skier. When I brought up being from Colorado, were you not prompted to tell me?"

"Think about it. Telling you would have probably prompted the same questions I just discussed. I realize it's silly. I do know the interest comes with good intentions, but it doesn't change the fact I find the whole back and forth content fucking frustrating."

"Yeah, that's probably true. Are you mad at me? Don't be mad at me."

"I'm not. Not at all. Just answering your curiosity as to why I didn't bring it up. So I'll tell you now. I do ski. Started at around three years old, and by about six I was putting the older kids to shame. In walking distance was a steep grassy hill, which packed a lot of snow. It was a common spot for all us kids and we loved to ski down it. It was our version of a bunny hill."

"That's what Erin said. I imagine for you to be as good as I was told, this hill most likely wasn't your only experience."

"You're right. I could hardly be considered fantastic if it were. Had a season pass to Jackson Hole. Are you familiar with the name?"

"Yes, I heard it has the most amazing ski resorts."

"True. I had a pass specifically for Snow King Resort. I'm sure Erin mentioned the name Ashlyn to you."

"She's involved in planning the reunion."

"Yes. Well, her parents also purchased family passes. We spent a lot of time there. Snow King Mountain is referred to as the 'Town Hill'. Always loved that. Anyway, her sister Haley and I used to alternate between skiing and tubing. Had so much fun."

"Sounds like it. Maybe we can go sightseeing there."

"Sure, but obviously you won't get the full effect without snow."

"Then we'll just have to come back this winter."

"I would love that. Maybe we could even travel to Colorado and visit where you skied."

"We can definitely do that."

"Great!" I yawned. "Sorry, didn't get much sleep last night. I never do before a trip."

"Understand. Get some rest and I'll let you know when we land."

"Thanks, I'm beat." As soon as I closed my eyes, I was out.

18

A NEIGHBORHOOD REUNION

Erin and I arrived at six o'clock as we'd been instructed. Erin had arranged for a driver, since the parking would be limited. We had the driver drop us off near our bunny hill. Erin paid the tip and we got out.

I walked over to the hill and looked up to the top. As I stood there in front of the hill, memories began to rise within me. The memories took over my sight and replaced the scene before me with visions of the past. Visions of a steep, snowy hill buzzing with activity. Visions of layers of clothing worn under a snowsuit. Visions of gloves tucked into sleeves and snowboots secured into skis. Visions of a long march up and quick ride down. Visions of making snowballs, leaving traces of snow chunks sticking to mittens. All these memories filled me with delight. I rejoined Erin and felt my face still beaming as she put her arm around me.

"Welcome home, Kerrie."

"It's nice to be back. Sorry for delaying us, Erin."

"Quite all right. I called Ashlyn and she said our timing is perfect. They were running behind schedule."

"I'm glad." A small path parted the woods beside my house, providing us with our route to and from the hill. I found it comforting to see the path still existed.

The house was just as I remembered. Everyone had gathered in the back, which was where we headed, and soon voices were calling our names. Ashlyn came out the back door and approached us with open arms.

"It is so good to see you both," said Ashlyn. "Haley is so excited to see you, Kerrie."

"Great to see you too, Ashlyn. Is Haley here?"

"Not yet. She's stuck in traffic, but should be here shortly. So, Erin tells me you stopped by the hill."

"Yeah, I was capturing the past. Great turn out, Ashlyn."

"It's amazing. Everybody was very receptive to the idea and quickly signed on to attend. Food is inside, and drinks are in the cooler over there. Help yourself, Kerrie. I am going to borrow Erin, if you don't mind."

"That's fine. I'll just walk around and mingle." I started to do that, when I made eye contact with my friend Kate. We instantly screamed out each other's names and exchanged hugs.

Here we were, back together again. Although many years had come between us, our friendship hadn't been lost. The same excitement we shared together as kids was still there. Without missing a beat, we broke into conversation.

"Hey Kerrie, remember when we were kids all bundled up in snowsuits? We could barely move, but still managed to make it up the hill with our tubes to slide down. We had our own private section, while the older kids took over the majority for skiing."

"Funny you should mention that. Erin and I had our driver drop us off at the hill so we could walk over here like old times. Anyway, I got out of the car and was drawn to it. Almost like in a hypnotic state. Found myself standing in front of the hill with flashes of memories flooding back. This was common ground for all our ages. The last memory before Erin and I headed over was of clumps of snow sticking to my mittens." We both giggled.

"Yeah, from making snowballs to hit the older kids as they were skiing down. Our form of revenge for teasing us." The teasing was never mean-spirited, but always fun.

"Well, that revenge wasn't very effective," I recalled. "We were so little and so stuffed into our snowsuits, the snowballs didn't go far. Mine didn't get much farther than the tips of my boots."

"That may be so, but you sure could ski. I used to enjoy you getting the better of the older kids. Left them in the dust." I smirked and gave a quick chuckle.

"Have to admit, I loved that too. I was a bit older and no longer layered, which gave me wiggle room suited for competition." We were not at a loss for words. I felt an arm rest on my ap

shoulder. Kate and I turned our heads to see Haley hugging both our necks.

We all screamed with the thrill of being together again after so many years of being apart. When we were little, Haley would sometimes come over and talk with us before hanging out with Emily. For a little while, anyway.

"Haley!" Kate and I simultaneously yelled out. Haley hugged us a little longer and then came around front to face us.

"Cannot believe I'm seeing you two." She teared up with joy, which got me choked up.

We talked for a bit, then Kate said, "I'm going to grab a soda. Can I bring you both back something?"

"I'm good," I replied. "Thanks, though."

"A bottled water. Thanks, Kate." Haley looked at me with disbelief. "Kerrie, you are all grown up. Oh my gosh, we were both kids when we last saw each other. Always considered you my little sister, and then you were taken from me."

"Never knew you felt that way. I always thought you were cool to let me hang out with you. You know, when I would come to your house."

"Right. I loved that." We saw Kate heading back with the drinks. Haley took her water. "I'm going to look for Ashlyn and give you two more of a chance to catch up. I'll talk to you both later." Before she could leave, Emily came up and grabbed Haley's arm and looked at me.

"Hey Kerrie, glad you made it. It's so great seeing Kate and you together again."

"Thank you, Emily. Nice to see Haley and you together as well. This is just like old times." With a smile, she pulled Haley away and I heard them giggling. That familiar, contagious laugh of Haley's entered my ears. It was just Kate and I again, like when we were younger. We had mixed with other friends, but for the most part hung out alone. We had always had fun and laughed constantly. Sometimes we found it hard to stop. I would laugh so hard my stomach hurt.

"Did you mention Erin being with you?" asked Kate. "I would love to see her again."

"Let's go look for her." Along the way, we stopped and mingled with other guests, most of whom we had never spoken to before but were now connecting with for the first time. All of us shared our childhood memories and answered questions about our current lives.

Overwhelmed by the attendance, I had forgotten there was food until we started to step inside. I'd gotten just one foot in the door when Tess approached me. "Kerrie, I'm so glad you made it. You're back at your first home. How does it feel?"

"Fantastic! I was glad to hear you purchased the house, Tess. I feel as if it's stayed in the family this way. It's like all of us are part of one big extended family."

"That's exactly how I feel. And looking around, I believe everyone here shares this same opinion. Sorry, come in. I didn't mean to keep you in the doorway. Let me take you on a tour."

"Awesome!" Kate and I followed Tess, and heard Erin calling out to me. We all stopped and saw Erin making her way through the crowd toward us.

"Kate was wanting to see you, Erin," I said. She finally reached us and stood there staring at Kate and me.

"Seeing you standing there together is incredible. You were little kids when my family moved away. Were so adorable and still are." Erin looked at us a little longer and then faced Tess. "Tess, the place looks fabulous. Sorry to interrupt."

"Thank you, Erin. And no problem. Would you like to join the tour?"

"Sure." Erin wrapped her arm through Kate's. "Hang back with me, Kate, and tell me what's been going on. I see enough of Kerrie as it is."

The tour continued, with Tess pointing out minor changes, none of which had changed the house's essence. As we headed up the stairs, I remembered where each room was and knew my bedroom was just around the corner.

I stepped inside my old room and felt like Alice. I wondered if the room had shrunk over the years, because I remembered it as so much bigger. We moved on to the other bedrooms. "I agree with Erin, Tess. Everything looks fabulous," I said. We finished the tour and Tess excused herself to mix with her other guests. I thanked her and headed straight for some food. Erin and Kate were still talking.

Grabbing a plate, I headed around the table to collect samples of just about everything. I would have tried it all, but my plate soon ran out of space. It was probably for the best, given the assortment of desserts I had noticed in the kitchen while on the house tour. I sat down with my food and chatted some more.

After everone had gotten a bite and was feeling full, we decided to take a walk to the hill for old times' sake, just like Erin and I had done when walking over here. We needed time for our stomachs to settle before we began attacking the desserts. Our unified return to the path was an indescribably surreal moment. Several people took pictures, and many were deep in conversation. Once the cameras stopped flashing, Tess invited us back for dessert and coffee.

The evening continued into the wee hours of the morning. As kids, we had been in separate groups of friends, divided by age. The reunion melted all those divisions so that we were one big group. As adults, we were now united by a singular memory of a happy childhood. There was a shared desire to stay in touch. The reunion would ultimately end, but our connections didn't have to. With that in mind, the event did not conclude with a goodbye, but rather with something like a "to be continued."

19

THE FOLLOWING DAY

I slept in, since it was actually morning when my head hit the pillow. I knew we were heading back today but, with the luxury of Kirk's plane, we didn't have to be on a schedule. I got up and was about to leave my room, when I saw Erin sitting on the sofa reading a magazine. Stopping in the doorway, I stretched my arms and legs by standing on tiptoes and reaching my hands toward the ceiling. "When are we heading back?" I asked. Erin looked up from her magazine.

"We're not." Her answer took me by surprise, because she'd been so intent on getting back to Davide. I didn't quite know how to respond.

"Excuse me? I thought you were anxious to see Davide again." Erin was about to answer, when there was a knock on the door. She went over and opened it, letting Ashlyn and Haley in. They were carrying beer and donuts. Haley handed out the beer while Ashlyn held the box of donuts.

"Did you tell Kerrie what's going on?" asked Ashlyn.

"Haven't had a chance," replied Erin. "And besides, I'm not really clear on what's going on, as you put it. All you told me was you needed us to stay an extra day. Oh, and that you had something to tell us. Does Haley know?"

"Hello, I'm standing right here, Erin, and no I don't," said Haley, jokingly. Despite this jovial mood, a nervous energy filled the room. In the midst of this rapid-fire exchange, I could not get a word in edgewise. Finally, Erin and Haley moved to the sofa, which gave me an opening, and I waved my hand.

"I am here, also, and you all are acting way too cryptic. What is going on?" Haley and Erin both shrugged their shoulders at me. "Ashlyn, tell me what, exactly?"

"Hey, Kerrie, you might want to sit down." A request to sit down was not generally a good sign, and the thought of sitting made me anxious.

"You're really scaring me. Think I'd rather stand."

"Might be better if you sit down."

"Believe I'd still prefer to stand, if that's all right."

"Then at least stand closer to Erin and Haley." I was still standing in the doorway, and figured she wanted to be able to face us all at the same time. I walked over, stood beside the sofa, and placed my beer on the end table. The sitting area was nice and spacious, which wasn't surprising, since Kirk had made the arrangements. A loveseat was positioned on one side of the sofa, and a recliner chair was on the other side.

"What the fuck, Ashlyn," Erin interjected, "you're scaring me, too. Are you okay? You know you're my dearest friend, and you are making me very concerned."

"I'm sorry, that was not my intention."

"Put the donuts down in the kitchen," said Erin. "Then come back and talk to us." You could hear a pin drop as we waited for Ashlyn's return.

"I don't know how to begin. Guess there's no way to ease into this. Might just have to blurt it out."

"Then fucking blurt it out already," Haley said.

"Yeah," Erin agreed. "What Haley said."

"Okay. Okay." Ashlyn looked into the eyes of Erin and then Haley. When she got to me, her eyes didn't meet mine. I couldn't help but notice.

"Did I do something wrong, Ashlyn?" I asked. Ashlyn finally looked into my eyes.

"No. No. Not at all." Haley crossed her arms and began tapping her foot.

"Ashlyn," shouted Haley, "for crying out loud, get on with it." Ashlyn remained focused on me. I was now wishing she wasn't.

"Kerrie, your mother is alive." I couldn't comprehend what she had just said. I was speechless.

"What in the hell are you talking about, Ashlyn?" asked Erin.

"Fuck!" said Haley.

"I don't understand," I said. "My mother died years ago." I couldn't think of anything else to say.

"No, she didn't."

I felt extremely nauseous. Color left the room, and blackness closed in on me. Then I felt my arms being rubbed and hands being squeezed, and heard voices that seemed to be coming from a distance.

I tried to open my eyes in response to everyone calling out my name, but couldn't. My inability was disconcerting. They were not speaking to each other, but rather were all focused on getting my attention. I didn't know how long it was before I could open my eyes or, for that matter, how much time had passed while I was out cold.

My eyes opened to the three of them looking down at me. I suddenly felt a cold compress on my forehead and reached up to touch it. By then, I was wishing I was Dorothy, and they were about to tell me I had just had a bad dream. I couldn't fathom any other alternative. Seriously, how could this be possible?

20

THE EXPLANATION

Lying on the loveseat, I held the compress to my head. Erin and Haley resumed their spots on the sofa. Ashlyn angled the chair and sat down so that we all faced her. My intent to learn the truth allowed me to regain focus. "I am aware you all probably have a million questions," began Ashlyn. "Who wants to start?"

Haley jumped right in. "I do. How was I not aware of this? We're sisters." Ashlyn and Haley were three years apart.

"Haley, I'll tell you how I found out, and that should explain it. We were both in college and working at the time. This would have been your first year. I came home earlier than expected. Dad was on the phone in the kitchen. I overheard him say, 'Kerrie is doing well, Meg. Your dad has just started her working in the pub with him.'" My mother's name was Margaret, but she was often called "Meg" by those closest to her.

"Oh my goodness! That's why you always wanted to go to the pub," Erin said. "You were checking on Kerrie."

"What the fuck, Erin," I blurted. "You never told me about coming to the pub."

"That's because I feared it would open up questions I didn't know the answers to. I always suspected from the way Ashlyn acted that she was keeping something from me. She was all cloak and dagger, observing our surroundings with a heightened awareness, as if incognito. We always told each other everything, but since she wasn't offering, I wasn't asking. I had a sickening sense that whatever it was, it could not be good. I wondered about you but, under the circumstances, thought it best to keep my concerns to myself, on the off chance this secrecy really was related to you. Seems I was right."

"Fair enough," I said.

"Sorry, Erin," responded Ashlyn. "I always felt bad about that, but I just couldn't."

"Understand." Erin looked back at me. "Anyway Kerrie, I was at the pub, but never did see you. At least I don't think so. Wouldn't have known what you looked like. And besides, I wasn't even aware you lived in the above apartment until our recent conversation, so I'd have no reason to think you'd be there. I recognized your grandfather, though, because of the front stoop story I told you about. However, the timing never seemed right to talk to him, which I know now was probably for the best."

"I remember that," Ashlyn said. "He would call us over to tell us jokes and stories when we were hanging out at the cul-de-sac. We all ran to join him on the stoop."

"Right," Erin said. "Now, let's get back to where you left off. You overheard your dad mention Kerrie. Then what?"

"Well, obviously I couldn't believe what I'd heard, and wished I hadn't. I held back in the family room until my dad hung up. He had a startled expression when I entered the kitchen."

"I can imagine," Haley said. "Especially since dad was the one who sat us down to tell us Mrs. Brannon had died. He didn't offer more than that, and we didn't ask."

"That's all my mom told me," said Erin. "It was obvious to me none of them had ever discussed the news with each other. It was also abundantly clear we were all in need of some enlightenment."

"Well, then," Ashlyn said, "you can imagine how shocked I was, and seeing my dad's startled face did not help. I'm sure it didn't help him any to see mine. He sat me down and told me I must not tell anyone what he was about to say." Ashlyn then paused. The room was quiet with anticipation.

"Kerrie, I think the best way to continue would be for you to tell me what you remember, and I'll fill in the gaps. Do you think you're up to it?" I sat up to face everyone and collect my thoughts on how to begin.

"Actually, I remember the events vividly. I recently shared them with Erin, so they're fresh in my mind. I'll give you a condensed version. My mother went out for the evening. I was catching lightning bugs out front, when a police officer showed up. He quietly engaged my grandfather in a conversation. Afterward, my grandfather put his head down, looked in my direction, and called me over as the officer was leaving. He told me my mother had been in a car accident and died.

"The bluntness seems kind of cold now. In fairness, I think sugar coating it might have made it too subtle for me to be able to grasp. This is actually a moot point, since my mother didn't die. The point was my grandfather needed me to believe she had. I am struggling to make sense of what the reason possibly could have been." I was stuck on this thought, as it kept repeating itself in my head. My mind worked through the events in reverse until a realization struck me.

"Wait!" Based on the shocked looks I received, my voice must have been loud compared to my previous silence. "Rewinding the events of that day, it occurs to me that my understanding of my mother's death, through all these years, was based solely on the belief that my grandfather had told me exactly what the officer had told him. I had no cause not to take him at his word, till now. With that in mind, I now realize he concocted a pretty elaborate ruse.

"I recall him sitting me down the next day to explain that there was going to be a private burial and that Mrs. Tyler from next door would be looking after me. 'Funerals are no place for a child,' he insisted. My grandfather's reason for lying most likely came from what the officer had actually said. This is what I'm missing. I found the gap, as you put it."

"Yes. That's it, Kerrie. The police officer was a friend of the family. He even dated your mother in high school."

"Didn't know any of that."

"I gathered. The fact you never mentioned him with any familiarity was a clue. Anyway, the police officer's name was Frank, and he spoke to your grandfather as a courtesy. Your mother was being held in jail on a DUI charge. She had been pulled over for reckless driving and appeared to be extremely agitated. Even threatened to assault the arresting officer by waving her fist in his face. Frank happened to be at the station when your mother was brought in." I hung on to every word.

"After you fell asleep, your grandfather called our house and my dad answered. He was aware my parents had stayed in touch with your mother after you both moved in. I'll now tell you what I was told. Don't hesitate to stop me if you need to."

"Thank you, but I don't think that will be necessary. I'm anxious to hear what you have to say." Erin and Haley seemed just as eager to hear the rest of the story.

"Your grandfather expressed appreciation for the support shown for his daughter. He'd been aware for some time that my father had known of your mother's difficulties, but he was pretty certain my father hadn't known their extent. Your grandfather kept hoping things would get better, but told my father this latest incident was the last straw. He admitted telling you she'd been in a car accident and died. With the assistance of Frank, arrangements were made to transport your mother from the jail to a psychiatric facility for evaluation. Your grandfather requested my dad's help in you not finding out. You were his responsibility now, and he felt it necessary, for your well being, that you believed your mother was dead.

"Your grandfather confessed he had made mistakes with your mother growing up. It pained him to witness the damage your mother was causing you as a result of those mistakes. He couldn't change the past with your mother and realized he could not even undo the damage done to you, but he hoped to provide you with a happier future.

"He saw this as an opportunity to make things right, in a way. Like he was being given a second chance to raise a child, but this time could do a better job. He did not know how long the facility would hold your mother, but he told my father he would consider it a favor to him if my parents continued to stay in touch with her once she was released.

"That's it, Kerrie. Everything that happened that day, anyway. I will tell you this, though, your grandfather did not elaborate on the damage to you. You don't have to tell us if you don't want to. Now, there is something I want to share with you." Ashlyn got up and walked over to me, tears in her eyes.

"Kerrie, I've always had the utmost respect for your grandfather, which is why I honored his wishes to keep this secret. He was awfully proud of you, and would light up at the mere mention of your name." At these words, I teared up also.

"I had the privilege of seeing what a fine job your grandfather was doing when Erin and I visited the pub. I look at you now and see what a fine job he did, but that's just it. You're all grown up, and I felt it was time for you to know and make a choice for yourself on how to proceed. I just hope your grandfather is looking down and nodding his head in agreement."

Ashlyn bent down and gave me a hug. "I love you, Kerrie. I'm here if you need me." Ashlyn returned to her seat. I managed to hold back the tears until she sat down. Now they were streaming down my face. I looked around and saw Erin and Haley had been affected in the same way. There wasn't a dry eye in the room.

"It's gonna be a double session with my shrink this week," Erin said. We all busted out laughing. "My fucking mascara ran so much I need to chase it with my beer." Now the tears streaming down our faces were from laughing so hard.

"Leave it to you, Erin," said Haley. "You always have a way of bringing a blue sky to a cloudy day." We continued to laugh, because Haley was so right. It was Erin's gift.

I would have said Haley was just as funny as Erin. Once Haley and Erin's banter got to going, you might as well sit down and settle in for a comedy routine. Haley had made a career out of her humor. She was a screenwriter for a highly successful comedy series. Ashlyn was also funny, especially after a few drinks, when she was more relaxed. When she'd been drinking, she started dropping the "F-bomb," which was hilariously out of character for her. The rest of us had such fluency with the word that it basically rolled off our tongues. The pressures of Ashlyn's job kept her in a serious mode, difficult to break free of. Ashlyn had her own business as a party planner to the rich and famous. Her specialty was planning parties around a theme. Each of us had made a name for ourselves in the celebrity world.

"Well, then," Ashlyn said, "does anybody have anything to add or questions to ask? Can't believe you don't."

"I have plenty to say, but first we need to eat something," said Erin. "Is anyone else hungry?" Everybody agreed that they could eat. Ashlyn looked at me.

"Kerrie, I know this is a lot to process," she said. "You don't look so good. Are you all right?"

"Sure. Just feeling a little tired is all."

"Kerrie, that's understandable," said Erin.

"Yes," agreed Haley. "I'm definitely here for you, little sis, as we all are."

"True dat," said Erin. "Whatever you need."

"All of you have been swell, and I'm comforted by your friendship. Thanks for everything." They all smiled at me in response, but I knew they were also hoping to cover up their concern.

"Get some rest, Kerrie," said Ashlyn.

"Okay. Would you mind if I lie down?"

"Not at all," said Erin. "In fact, I feel like cooking. We'll go to the store and pick up a few groceries while you're sleeping. We'll take the donuts with us to tide us over. That should give you plenty of time to rest. We'll resume talking after we eat."

"Thanks, Erin. An hour is probably all I'll need. Then I'll be ready for that talk." Haley collected her beer and shook Erin's to find it was empty.

"You drive, Erin, 'cause I'm going to finish off my beer and grab another for sustenance with the donuts." This was classic Haley, and we all roared in unison.

After they closed the door, I headed straight for my pillow. I didn't expect I would take long to fall asleep. My head already felt heavy from lack of sleep, the kind of feeling that strikes suddenly after you've been on the go too long. Hugging my pillow, I closed my eyes.

21

OLD FAMILY RECIPE

I took a shower and got dressed. I'd quickly fallen into a sound sleep and was now fully rested. A scent from the kitchen pulled me out of my room and I joined the others.

"Smells delicious, Erin," I said.

"Thanks, Kerrie," she said. "Thought I'd make your favorite dish. Told you I would sometime. Today seemed like a fitting day to make good on that promise."

"You made eggplant parmesan? Wow! I don't even remember sharing that with you."

"Yep. I'm not likely to forget any conversation where Italian food is the topic. It's an old family recipe. Figured we could all use some comfort food."

"Awesome! My mouth is watering."

"Are you feeling any better?" asked Ashlyn. "Can I get you anything?"

"I'm fine. I feel much better. I was able to fall into a sound sleep, so I'm feeling fully rested."

"It seemed like you were," said Ashlyn. "I checked on you when we got back."

"Yeah, heard you were all back before I hopped in the shower. Sorry I slept so long." Haley noticed me eyeing their glasses of wine and handed me one. We all clinked our glasses and had a seat around the table.

"You needed to sleep. Besides, the meal's prep time took a while," Erin said. "You slept through most of the cook time, as well. The food only has about thirty minutes left."

"Perfect," I said. Haley stood up and took my arm.

"Come on, Kerrie. Let's see what we can find on TV."

After we'd eaten dinner and cleaned up, we gathered around the sitting area to continue our previous conversation.

"Okay, Erin," Ashlyn began, "what was it you wanted to say?"

"Changed my mind. I think it's more important Kerrie goes first. I'm sure she has some questions to ask. Have you had enough time to absorb it all yet?"

"There is one thing I took note of. Ashlyn, you mentioned my grandfather didn't elaborate on my damage. I noticed you did not include the mistakes he referred to in that statement, and got the impression you know what they are. Am I right?"

"Very astute of you, Kerrie. I do know. Are you sure you want me to go into all that?"

"Yes. I think maybe it will help me understand my mother, which I need to be able to do."

"Okay. Your grandfather shared his past to reveal his mistakes. He spoke of being an alcoholic. He felt the need to clarify he was not a mean drunk, which is often associated with the disease, but was your typical life-of-the-party, happy drunk. Regardless, he blamed himself for your mother's troubles by admitting to spending more time with the bottle than with her.

"Little girls generally idolize their fathers, and your mother definitely fell into this category. She began acting out at a young age just to get your grandfather's attention. She had gotten plenty from your grandmother, but it was his she was seeking. Her bad behavior resulted in your grandfather getting help for his drinking and spending more time with her.

"Guess it was a classic case of too little, too late. Your mother's behavior never improved, it only became more demanding. In the beginning, your grandfather gave into her in an attempt to make up for his alcoholism. Continued to do so because it was a quick and easy way to put an end to her tantrums.

"Ended up making the situation worse by enabling the demanding behavior, which became stronger as she grew older. Your mother wanted total attentiveness, making life in the home exceedingly difficult. Your grandparents gained a moment's peace at their own expense.

"After your parents met and were married, it appeared your mom had improved. This is what your grandfather wanted to believe, anyway. Didn't know what happened between your parents, but he knew something triggered your mother's relapse. Having you move in allowed him to keep close tabs on your life and attempt to make it better for you both.

"This is all I know. Maybe you know what happened between your parents. Did this help at all?"

"Actually did. As far as my parents split, I'm reminded of something that happened when I was nine. Came home from school and entered the kitchen.

"My mother was sitting at the far end of the table in the dark. At the time, this did not strike me as odd, being a clueless kid and all. She said she had a question to ask me, and emphasized that if I told the truth there would be no punishment. I remember feeling concerned. I often acted without thinking, which got me into trouble at home.

"For example, one time I'd picked flowers out of a yard on the way home. They looked pretty, and I thought the bouquet would be a nice gift for my mother. I walked inside the house with the flowers securely hidden behind my back in order to surprise her, hoping she'd be pleased. My mother met me at the door with a question that started with, 'Did you?' That's all I needed to hear to know my answer probably should have been no.

"As you would expect, the question was about my picking the flowers. Being more than happy to oblige, I answered "No" while holding the items in question behind my back.

"Now, faced with another question, my mind began to race through all my recent actions, trying to figure out what I had done, to no success. I looked up and my mother asked, 'Did you tell Mrs. Davies your father and I were getting a divorce?'

"I felt immediate relief, because I truly had not. Divorce wasn't even in my vocabulary because, as you know, nobody we knew had experienced it. I proudly said 'No' and was sent to my room.

"The next weekend my grandparents came over, as they usually did when my parents went away. Because it was a normal occurrence, I didn't suspect a thing.

"I came home from Kate's one afternoon and my mother was back, but my father wasn't. My grandfather took me aside to explain my parents were splitting up. He informed me my mother and I would be moving in with him and my grandmother.

"Years later, I recounted this story to a therapist with an awareness that sitting in the dark had been significant. My therapist acknowledged that I was correct, and through psychoanalysis interpreted what she believed really took place. According to her, my mother was probably sitting there with a fear of divorce looming. My therapist inferred that when I entered the room, my mother projected that fear onto me by merely asking the question."

"That's wild," said Haley. "I know what you said about divorce not being in your vocabulary because none of us had been exposed to it either directly or indirectly. Therefore, you never told Mrs. Davies, and obviously she would have had no cause to speak with your mother about it. I get all that, but still can't help but think your mother believed her own accusation."

"You're absolutely right, on two counts. One, the question was more of an accusation. Two, it was a case of blurring the lines between thought and reality, with fear being the culprit in this instance. It's as if simply speaking the thought out loud somehow made it true."

"Very profound, Kerrie," said Erin.

"Yes, and I didn't know you were in therapy," said Ashlyn, with a tone of surprise.

"Yeah. Probably should explain the timing so it makes sense. You said your father mentioned I had just started working in the pub. I imagine you and Erin visited shortly after. Am I right?"

"Yes," she answered.

"Thought so. Anyway, I was fine at that point. I had recently become interested in reading and even started dabbling in writing. Writing gave me a purpose. I was a train wreck before that. My grandfather had me committed to rehab, which is where I received therapy and where those interests began. After I was discharged and got settled back in, my grandfather started me working with him."

"What sort of rehab, if you don't mind me asking?" said Haley.

"Strictly marijuana. Started dabbling in eighth grade, but my use increased when I began high school and became even more frequent my sophomore year. I had no money to buy my own supply, so was at the disposal of friends offering it. In high school, this never proved to be a problem. Especially once I could drive."

"Did drinking become a problem for you like it was for your grandfather?" asked Ashlyn.

"Never. Didn't see the point of drinking when my needs were met more quickly with smoking. Still don't have a need to drink in excess, unless I'm upset and trying to get over it. Even so, it's only a brief digression."

"So, I'm assuming your rehab occurred when you were a sophomore," said Haley.

"Yeah. The summer after. Ended up having to repeat tenth grade."

"Getting back to your parents, Kerrie," said Erin, "do you have any idea what happened between them?"

"Think I might be able to guess from what Ashlyn shared about my grandfather, combined with my own experience.

"Once we moved in with my grandparents, my mother's scrutiny transferred from my father to me. Any failure to comply with the standards my mother demanded brought on a barrage of harsh criticism. My father must have had enough. This became my life." Everyone faced me, silent. I couldn't stop talking. As old emotions surfaced, I couldn't stop turning them into words.

"I internalized the guilt I felt from failing to consistently meet my mother's needs. I lacked the tools necessary to handle the negativity surrounding my mother's inability to cope. In other words, I couldn't rise above my own hurt, but always thought I should be able to. A persistent feeling of powerlessness caused by the hurt, combined with my mother's expectations, badgered me. Because she was, after all, my mother. The guilt consumed my existence, leaving me in constant torment. This battle often prompted me to isolate myself in my room and seek solace within complete darkness and silence.

"My confidence shriveled away along with my identity. I had difficulty finding a way out. My body language must have revealed me as lost, which no doubt my grandfather saw, causing him the pain he spoke of. It only deepened after my mother's supposed death." I had come full circle, possibly answering what had happened between my parents, and definitely explaining the damage caused me. I sensed the wheels turning in my friends' minds.

"Kerrie," said Erin, "in all you said, what strikes me the most is the similarity to your mother in isolating yourselves in darkness and silence. The way I see it, the difference comes from your ability to deeply appreciate love and laughter, which enables you to fully experience both."

"Wow! You're right. Can't believe I never made the connection. Even in sharing, it still didn't occur to me." I pondered this, but only for a moment, because the question that soon came from Haley registered with me. I always considered the delay between hearing and comprehending similar to what foreign correspondents experienced with their delayed responses.

"Did using drugs replace your need for isolation?"

"Yeah. Drugs acted as a bandage masking my anguish, which led me to stupidly believe I had everything under control. Didn't realize I had just exchanged one issue for another. Thought of it more as a chosen path to relief. It all seemed perfectly logical, because had my ache been physical, there'd be no qualms about self-medicating with aspirin."

"'Seemed' being the operative word," said Haley. "You look great, Kerrie. Rehab must have done the trick."

"Thanks. I learned from therapy that the responsibility I felt for my mother's happiness was pointless, because she had to be responsible for her own well being. My reactions were understandable, but to stay on that course of behavior was the root of the problem. I was instructed not to confuse explanations for excuses."

"What does that mean, exactly?" asked Erin.

"The problems we face can be used to explain our automatic reactions but are never an excuse for carrying on the poor behavior exhibited as a result of not coping.

"Two types of personality traits were described to me. One was lashing out in order to draw people in, yet ultimately pushing them away. The other was to withdraw and push people away, which usually drew them in. The first seldom can be helped, because there is either a lack of awareness of a problem existing or vehement refusal to even acknowledge the possibility. Can't help those not willing to help themselves. The second description carries the necessary awareness along with a desire to feel better. I was told this fit me."

"Well, that's for sure," agreed Erin. I chuckled.

"Guess you've experienced the latter with me. If no one has anything else to say, then the only information left to find out is where my mother is."

"Right," said Ashlyn, "but I do have one question I've been holding back asking. Why did you, being a child, feel responsible for your mother's happiness?"

"I suppose those times I witnessed my ability to make her happy translated into its being a reasonable expectation of me."

"I can see how that can easily happen." Ashlyn reached for her purse and handed me the address. "Your mother lives in a retirement community with a woman named Hazel."

"Hazel," I said.

"Yes. Do you know her?"

"Not sure. My mother had a friend, Hazel, from high school. They were best friends."

"Yes. They are one and the same. Turns out Hazel went to nursing school after they graduated, and is presently working as a hospice nurse. Your grandfather remained close friends with Hazel's parents, so he was aware of her occupation.

"Your grandfather contacted Hazel regarding your mother and enlisted her help to stay in touch. He had just heard your mother was to be released. Hazel had recently moved into a home in a brand-new community, and with the house next door available, she suggested they could be neighbors.

"The timing couldn't have been more perfect, and your grandfather made all the arrangements. He was very emphatic with your mother about not contacting you. Another reason to tell you, since there is nothing keeping her from it now. She works from home as a bookkeeper. Your grandfather had plenty of connections through the pub to get her started. The business has grown from there."

"What are you going to do, Kerrie?" asked Erin.

"I can't very well ignore what I've been told. I'll attempt to see her tomorrow. Maybe stay with her and finish my book."

"Do you want me to go with you?" Erin said.

"Thanks, Erin. Get back to Davide. I'll be fine."

"Haley and I are here for you, Kerrie. In fact, we'll be right back." Ashlyn and Haley left the room and returned holding overnight bags. "Thought we could stay with you two. I want to make sure you're okay, and besides, it'll be fun."

"I'm okay, but would love to have your company." Haley found a movie for us to watch, but we kept dozing off while fighting to stay awake, and finally gave in.

22

TAXI

Arrived at the address written on the sticky note. The phone number was also on there, but I preferred to just show up. Entered the number in my phone, though. I got out of the taxi and took a deep breath. The driver removed my belongings and brought them up to the house. When he returned, I paid, and he took off. A neighbor's door opened up, and a woman dressed in scrubs stepped out onto her porch. "Kerrie, is that you?"

"Yes, Hazel. It's me." I walked over and gave her a hug.

"You look great. So pretty and all grown up. Ashlyn called and told me you were coming. I have been watching out for you."

"Is everything all right?" I asked.

"Everything is fine. Ashlyn and I felt, under the circumstances, it might be a good idea for you to have company visiting your mother."

"I appreciate that. I am feeling a bit nervous." Hazel put her arm around me, and we headed over.

"Perfectly understandable. I thought it best not to tell your mother, on the off chance you changed your mind."

"Good thinking. I did battle with that possibility this morning." We reached the door, and again I took a deep breath. Hazel opened the door. As I stepped into the house behind her with my bags, I felt my whole body stiffen.

"Meg!" Hearing her name caused my body to stiffen even more, if possible.

"Coming, Hazel." I looked up to see my mother appear in the entrance of the foyer. She stopped in her tracks upon seeing me. She was still beautiful, with her dark hair and dark eyes.

"Look who's here, Meg," said Hazel.

"Kerrie? I can't believe it! After all this time."

"Hi, Mom. Long story short, I was in town with Erin visiting old friends, and Ashlyn gave me your information. Hope you don't mind me dropping in like this." She motioned me closer and opened her arms for a hug. Following our embrace, she stepped back and held me at arm's length.

"Let me get a good look at you. All grown up." She turned and looked at Hazel. "Look how pretty my baby girl is."

"I know. Told her the same thing."

"Well, let's all go in the kitchen and have a seat."

"I have to go to work, Meg, but I'll check back later. Besides, it will give you two a chance to get caught up."

"Okay then, Hazel." Holding the screen door open to leave, Hazel paused in the doorway and smiled at us both before taking off.

My mother led me toward the kitchen. "Kerrie, you are staying the night?"

"Would you be all right if I did?" My mother headed to the refrigerator, and I sat down.

"Of course. Stay as long as you like. What can I get you to drink?"

"Iced tea, if you have some." She got a glass out of the cabinet, added ice, and poured tea from the pitcher. "I'm close to finishing my book and would like to stay until it's complete." My mother handed me the glass and I took a taste. I recognized my grandfather's recipe, but thought it best left unmentioned. She joined me after getting one for herself and placed the pitcher on the table for refills.

"How exciting. You've done well for yourself. I'm really proud of you. So, you mentioned being here with Erin. I assume you were visiting friends from our neighborhood, since you also spoke of Ashlyn." Because my mother had brought it up and because the majority of her time there had been good, I felt comfortable explaining.

"Yes, Ashlyn contacted Erin and me about a neighborhood reunion. It was this past Saturday, and an amazing number of us attended." My mother beamed while listening, probably recalling the good times we had had.

"That's lovely. We had such wonderful neighbors. I want you to tell me all about it." She had many questions about the event, and I gladly answered them.

The mood was friendly, but I kept waiting for the other shoe to drop. "Let me show you to your room," she eventually said. We both got up, and I followed her down the hall. I placed my bags on the bed and began to unpack.

"When you finish unpacking, come back to the kitchen and we'll have some dinner."

"Okay. Are you all right with me doing laundry while I'm here?"

"Sure. The laundry room is next door to your room."

"Perfect."

I took a bag of dirty clothes and started a load. By the time I returned, dinner was ready.

After dinner, I excused myself to work on the book, and my mother went into the family room to watch one of her favorite programs. I moved my laptop from the bed, set it up on the desk, and got started. The dryer's buzz stopped me at the end of a paragraph. I worked on removing clothes from the dryer as my mother headed down to her room.

"I'm going to call it a night, Kerrie. See you in the morning."

"Okay, Mom. Once I put my laundry away, I'll be going to bed." Once I finished my chore, I shut down the laptop and made a plan of trying to get a fresh start in the morning.

23

CRUNCH TIME

The party was over. The other shoe had dropped. It wasn't long before my mother reprised her desired role of being waited on. I fell back into a routine of attempting to fill all the orders being called out. No sooner had I headed in one direction than a new request took me in another. If I did not respond quickly enough, complaints and criticisms ensued. Her latest request required me to go to the store.

Before leaving the house, my mother called me back to critique my outfit. "Is that what you're wearing?"

"Yeah. What's wrong with it?"

"I'm sure you have plenty of nice outfits, and you're wearing that. The one you were wearing yesterday was lovely."

"These are my lounging clothes."

"Exactly!"

"I'm just running a quick errand, and this is comfortable."

"Always good to look your best. You never know who you'll run into. Go change and I'll come with you." My mother had always had a penchant for harping on a point until I gave in. I had wasted time by insisting on my point, and now she was coming with me. So much for a quick errand. I changed clothes and went back to my mother to model the outfit.

"Much better. You could stand to wear some makeup, though." I opened my mouth and immediately closed it. Turned around and entered the bathroom to apply my makeup. Returned, and finally met with my mother's approval.

"While we're out, let's go shopping and get you more clothes. I'm sure you didn't pack enough." She was determined to be back in charge of my life. The ability to control was her drug. It had only taken a day to get back to this place.

We went to the mall, where my mother ran into several people she knew. I was introduced, and this time didn't just smile. Not only did I verbally respond, but I also extended my hand. I looked at my mother to catch her reaction. She gave me a pleased nod and a grin. This made me feel good. My mother insisted on paying for my new clothes. It was as if we had turned back time and were finishing our day of shopping. Several hours passed and we had yet to run our errand, but I accepted my decreased writing time because it had been a great day.

I had planned on staying with my mother for a week, because I had estimated it would be plenty of time to complete the book. Despite the interruptions, I was still intent on keeping the week as a deadline. In order to make it all work, I had to find a better way of managing my time.

The day flew by. Entering the house, I was confronted with both the necessity of getting back to writing and an extreme tiredness. Some of the tiredness was left over from my earlier efforts to work between tasks. I would never finish at the rate I was going, but I had to try. I needed to restore some of my energy so I could work through the night. I thought of brewing a pot of coffee, but felt a headache starting. A slight twinge above my right eye directed me to the bathroom to ward off a full-blown migraine.

I grabbed a bottle of aspirin from the medicine cabinet and poured out four pills, my usual dosage to knock out the twinge and prevent it from getting worse. I removed a Dixie cup, filled it with water, and swallowed the pills.

Putting back the aspirin, I was curious about what my mother was taking, and began reading prescription labels. I ran across a full bottle, which I took to ask her about. I couldn't understand why she wouldn't take a medication.

I headed for the kitchen to make some coffee. If it would help me stay awake, I'd drink straight out of the pot and save a cup.

My mother was sitting at the table balancing her checkbook.

"Hey Mom, what's this?"

"What's what?" she asked. I held out the bottle for her to read. "Oh, that. I don't sleep at night, and then I'm tired during the day. The doctor prescribed those so I'd have more energy during the day. What I need is sleeping pills. Forgot I even had them. Why?"

"Just curious as to why you wouldn't take a medication, and want to make sure you're taking care of yourself."

"I do. I'm good at taking my other medications, but didn't see the point in taking those when I really need something to help me sleep at night."

"I see what you're saying." I let my mom get back to the checkbook and prepared my coffee. Seeing her absorbed in her checkbook made me believe I could safely sneak off to my room. Finally, an opportunity to return to my laptop had arrived. Or so I thought.

"Before you leave, can you fix me some tea?" This was not a question, as it seemed to be. I put down my mug and went to the cabinet in search of one for her. "Where are you going?"

"To get you a coffee cup."

"I use one of those on the rack beside the microwave." I unhooked a cup and located a pot to heat water. "What are you doing with that pot?"

"I was going to use it to heat the water for the tea."

"Oh, I don't do all that. Just put water in the cup and heat it in the microwave." While the water was heating, I froze, not knowing where my mother kept the tea. "What's wrong? Why are you just standing there?" Turning around, I spotted a canister with the word "Tea" written on it. I didn't know if this was a trick or not. It seemed too easy, and made me suspicious.

I thought, "What the fuck," and went for it. I removed the lid and pulled out a tea bag. Holding it up, I asked, "Is this the tea?"

"Of course it is. What else would it be?" I prepared the tea according to her specifications, put the cup down beside her, and mistakenly thought I was good to go. "Need a little sugar." I recalled seeing another canister labeled "Sugar."

I confidently picked it up off the counter and brought it to the table with a spoon. "Not that." She pointed a finger back toward the counter. "It's the packets in the little wicker basket over there." I returned the canister and followed the direction of her finger. I successfully retrieved and delivered the basket. She ripped open a packet and poured it in. Exhaustion struck me as I watched her take a sip.

"Now it's not hot anymore." That meant it was no longer scalding.

"Want me to heat it up for you?" I asked.

"No. I'll do it." I felt for sure this was a trick. I had it all played out in my head, even. I would respond, "Okay," and she'd tell me how she knew I hadn't really wanted to do it.

"I really don't mind."

"That's okay. I know you're anxious to get back to working on your book."

"It won't take long, and then I can get back to my book."

"I'll get it. Go on."

"Are you sure? Still don't mind."

"Yes, I'm sure." With that, I stepped one foot forward. "Oh! Before you take off, just pick up the garbage and place it in the trash can in the garage. Then roll it down to the end of the driveway. Tomorrow is garbage day." Without responding, I detached the trash bag from a drawer and hustled.

Returning to the house, I quietly opened and closed the door. I couldn't do anything about the obnoxious loudness of the garage door as it closed. Relieved to hear the television, I stealthily moved to the opposite end of the house to my room. I kept the light off because of the headache I had experienced earlier. Then I remembered the coffee I had made. I opened up the laptop and attempted to push on without it.

Hoping to jump-start my writing, I read through the last page I had written. I found it extremely hard to concentrate. While struggling to get through the page, my head dropped.

I decided to change into my pajamas and splash cold water onto my face. Even considered making more coffee. I flipped the light on and emptied my pockets. From my right pocket, I removed the prescription bottle. I'd meant to put it back but had gotten distracted.

As I held it in the palm of my hand, I thought of the reason my mother's doctor had prescribed her this medication. Looking at the label to check the expiration, I noticed a recent issue date.

I was eager to finish this book, and I knew my plan of working through the night would be my only chance to meet the deadline, especially given the constant interruptions I had faced that day. My mother had had no problems getting her bookkeeping done because she could work and give orders at the same time. There was no movement required with that. I, on the other hand, could not fill the orders and type at the same time.

The good feeling I got earlier from pleasing my mother renewed my childhood aspiration to make her happy. I knew this time I would need to work harder at dealing with my hurt feelings.

Anyway, I was totally exhausted and in need of a little energy. That, after all, was why the doctor had ordered the medication for my mother. She may have had no use for it, but I did. Didn't take much to talk myself into trying it. This could be the solution to my time management problem, I thought. Hopefully it would enable me to help my mother during the day and work through the night. I told myself I'd quit once the book was done. No harm in that.

24

DEADLINE

The weekend had arrived. It was Friday, and I had made plans to return home on Monday. The medication had been a lifesaver. The energy it provided kept me awake and focused. I'd even been feeling remarkably calm. Unfortunately, as with all things, the benefits didn't last forever. So, I had to increase the dose a tad. It was no biggie. I was a couple of days shy of completion, and then I wouldn't need to take any more. I had to thank Hazel, as well, for helping me meet the deadline.

Hazel had come over mid-week to check on us. Told me she had come by the day before, but nobody was there. I explained that we had gone shopping. She looked at me with concern and asked if I had been getting enough sleep. Assured Hazel I was fine, and accounted for my appearance by revealing I'd set a deadline for finishing my book and had worked through the night because I had to help my mother during the day. She offered to help my mother so I could also have the days available. Hazel had no assigned case at the moment and was taking some time off. I couldn't see where that would be a problem, since my mother liked Hazel. Figured, with their close friendship, she would enjoy Hazel's company.

I didn't see much of Hazel. Only from a distance when she came over, because I hightailed it to my room and remained there until I heard her call out when she was leaving. I resurfaced after she left.

Satisfied with my accomplishment, I decided to make breakfast. Before getting started, I washed down some pills, took a shower, and put on one of my new outfits. My mother's daily routine began with working on her bookkeeping at the dining room table, where she could spread out and sort all the paperwork. I approached my mother, exuding optimism.

"Good morning, Mom."

"Oh, that looks nice," she remarked, and buried herself back into her work. The compliment combined with a grin expressed her pleasure with me. And, again, this made me feel good.

"Thank you. Will you be ready to eat? Thought I would make French toast."

"Sounds good. Just let me know when it's done," she answered, without looking up. Walking toward the kitchen, I spotted Hazel opening the front door.

"Good morning, Kerrie," greeted Hazel.

"Yes, it is," I replied. "Thanks to you, I am close to finishing my book. About to make some breakfast. I hope you can join us."

"Wonderful. I would love to."

"Great! French toast is my specialty."

"Sounds delicious. Can I help?"

"I got it. Go visit with mom and I'll call you both when it's ready."

"Okay." Hazel walked over to my mother, and I began preparing breakfast. I cut up some cantaloupe, dividing the pieces into two bowls, and put them in the refrigerator for later. Moving onto the French toast, I mixed cinnamon into egg batter and dipped in bread slices. While the slices were cooking on the griddle, I added additional cinnamon where needed. "Breakfast is just about ready," I announced. Cutting the slices in half, I layered them on one side of each plate. In the empty space, I added the bowls of cantaloupe.

Hazel came in and had a seat, and my mother followed shortly after. I put the plates down and raced to fill glasses with orange juice. Then, after placing the glasses beside their plates, I raced off again to get coffee. "This is a nice surprise, Kerrie," my mother stated.

"Nicely done," said Hazel.

"Thank you. I hope you both like it."

"I'm sure we will," replied my mother. "Aren't you having any?"

"No. I'm not that hungry, but you both dig in and enjoy."

"Kerrie, you need to eat something. Looks like you're losing weight." Hazel remained quiet and continued eating.

"I will grab something later. Promise. Better get back to work. I've turned the corner and am nearing the end."

"What's wrong with you? Seem awfully jumpy."

"I told you. Almost finished with my book. Guess it's made me kind of anxious."

"No, that's not it. There is something else going on. Sit down, you're making me nervous." I got some water and sat down. They were both watching me like hawks. Needing to do something with my hands, I lifted the glass to take a sip. My hands began to shake, and I dropped the glass. I thanked goodness it didn't break.

"Sorry! I'll clean it up." I picked up the glass and put it in the sink.

"Kerrie! Tell me what's going on with you."

"Nothing. Just clumsy. I really need to get back and finish." I grabbed a dishrag to soak up the water off the table. "I will be better once I'm done. You'll see."

"Fine," my mother huffed, "leave it and go on then." I made a quick exit. "Promise me, you will eat later," my mother hollered.

"Promise," I yelled back. I sat down at the desk and booted up my laptop.

"Kerrie," called Hazel in a soft voice. I jumped.

"Sorry, Hazel. I didn't even hear you come in."

"That's all right. Could see you were deeply focused, and I apologize for interrupting, but I feel we need to talk. Didn't want to speak to you in front of your mother. Look, Kerrie, I know what you're doing."

"What do you mean?" I knew by the way Hazel had watched me at breakfast she suspected something, but I was counting on the slight chance she'd been mistaken. In other words, I hoped my mother had not discussed her medications with Hazel. No matter how unlikely, I clung to this imagined possibility.

"Your mother always gets her prescriptions filled and, because I'm a nurse, she always asks for my opinion." There it was. My balloon of hope had had a pin stuck in it. Might as well let her finish before I started my defense. "To be more specific, she asks me about the likelihood of the side effects and, up until the last one, has never had a problem taking any of them. You are taking your mother's Dextroamphetamine. It was prescribed for narcolepsy." Hazel spoke matter-of-factly, and didn't even ask me to verify.

"Okay Hazel. I could tell by the way you were watching me earlier you suspected something. My only hope was that you had no knowledge of her medications, but I had a sickening feeling that was not the case. I just needed a little boost to be able to meet my deadline. I'm almost there, and then I will quit taking them. Promise."

"You are right about me studying your behavior, and from what I saw, I am afraid that quitting will not be easy. I know the signs of tolerance, where doses are tweaked for the initial purpose of getting a boost, as you admitted, but later increased to reach a high. You're addicted, Kerrie."

"I am not addicted, just motivated. Stop worrying, Hazel. Like I said earlier, I will be better once I'm done. You'll see."

"Okay. I will leave you now, but know I'm here if you want to talk."

"I know, and thank you." Hazel left and I got back to it. Geared myself up for the long hours ahead by taking more pills.

25

STAYING TRUE

I typed at a good clip until my mind became blocked, bringing all thoughts to an abrupt end. I read my last sentence, stood up, and began to pace. Kept silently repeating the words in an attempt to regain my rhythm while desperately trying to concentrate. Even started saying the words out loud with the hope I'd be able to focus better by hearing myself speak them. As I repeatedly circled the room, a weight on my eyelids got heavier, and my skin felt clammy.

"Hey, babe." I quickly turned at the sound of Kirk's voice. Standing in the doorway were Kirk and Erin.

"What are you guys doing here? Wait. Let me guess. Hazel."

"Yes," answered Erin. "Hazel phoned Ashlyn, who in turn called me. Then I enlisted Kirk. She was concerned, and I can see why. You're pale, eyes are droopy, and you've lost weight. We know everything, Kerrie, and have come to get you." I had my hands tucked firmly in my pockets.

"I only need two more days. Then all will be back to normal. I have plans to return home on Monday. Can you give me till then?" Without thinking, I removed my hands to plead with them to let me stay. Once out of my pockets, my hands immediately began trembling. Saw the look of horror in Erin's eyes.

"Kerrie, you're scaring me, and you made a promise. Remember?" I could now see a sadness consuming her, and I felt horrible being the cause.

"Okay, Erin. You're right. I'll come home with you."

"Actually, Kerrie, arrangements have been made for you to receive treatment." I looked to Kirk, and he nodded in agreement.

"This is true, babe. I set it up. Want you to get the best care."

"Okay. Does my mother know?"

"No," answered Erin. "We will wait here while you go talk to her. Hazel is hanging out, in case you need her."

I found my mother cleaning her work off the dining room table.

"Hey, Mom."

"Kerrie, what's up? I met your friends. Well, Erin I knew. So good seeing her again. We had a nice chat, and she shared about meeting you at Universal Studios. Then she introduced me to Kirk. He is polite and very handsome."

"I'm glad you enjoyed speaking to them. Kirk has a private plane, and they've come to get me."

"Thought you planned on leaving Monday."

"I did, but." I was trying to figure out how to explain.

"But, what? And why are you shaking? Spit it out, Kerrie."

"Okay. Well, you obviously know I have been trying to finish my book."

"Yeah. What about it?"

"I was extremely tired and needed some help. I started taking the stimulants you were prescribed. You had no use for them, and I did. Planned on stopping once the book was finished.

Hazel caught on and made the call, which brought Erin and Kirk here. Hazel feels I'm addicted, but I disagree. Who knows? Maybe she's right. Anyway, arrangements have been made for me to get help."

"Well, that explains a lot," my mother responded, using a tone. Rage was back in her eyes, and she began waving a finger at me. "You did this on purpose!" My mother raised her voice at me. "You haven't changed one bit!"

"What do you mean?" I was confused.

"You know perfectly well what I mean, Kerrie Marie!" The use of my middle name was a dead giveaway of rough seas ahead. "This is your way of getting out of here earlier. When you first arrived, you were a big help to me. I thought things could be different between us. We were getting along well. When Hazel started helping me, I knew it was because you didn't want to. You care more about that damn book of yours than about me."

"I offered to help, Meg," Hazel chimed in.

"You come here and ignore me in my own home. That's rude, Kerrie. Hazel knows that you're rude." My mother looked at Hazel. "Right, Hazel? Remember when you first met Kerrie and she didn't say hello back? Want you to know I raised her better than that."

I couldn't believe that was still on my list of sins. Hazel was speechless. I didn't have much to say, either. I knew my mother was not being rational, so there was no point in attempting to defend myself. Her voice grew louder with every accusation.

"I always blamed you for your father leaving. I needed your father and you stole him. Things were fine between us. Then he began doting on you. Started you skiing at an early age, which was even more time spent away from me." My mother had gotten out of control with her yelling. She seemed to have lost consciousness of anybody outside of the two of us.

"Dad left me, too. Remember?"

"Yes, but I'm sure he stayed in contact while you were with your grandfather. And that's another thing. Even stole my own father from me." I stayed away from that one.

"Dad continued to pay for my snow resort pass. This was our only connection. We never saw each other. You saw him last."

"I don't believe you!" There was a brief silence, interrupted by my mother screaming for me to get out. Again, I realized my mother was being irrational, but knowing that didn't make the words hurt any less.

I turned and saw Erin and Kirk standing by the front door. They had moved there without being noticed. In my mind, I wanted to run out the door, but my strength had been zapped by all the anger unleashed on me.

I carefully started walking toward the door. I was shaking badly and feared my legs were going to give out. Kirk raced over and picked me up. I placed my arms around his neck and collapsed my head onto his shoulder. We reached the car. Kirk put me down so I could get in.

"Kerrie, wait!" I held onto the door as Hazel ran toward me.

"What is it, Hazel?"

"Just gave your mother a sedative and put her to bed. Anyway, I wanted to tell you how sorry I am." I looked Hazel in the eyes and saw her sadness.

"You have nothing to be sorry for. I am curious, though. Did you find me rude all those years ago?"

"Not at all. Thought of you as extremely shy, and your smile revealed a natural warmth. Just like your grandfather. But I actually do have reason to feel responsible for this mess."

"Thank you, Hazel. Always wondered how you truly felt. And I doubt it."

"I was with your mother that night and knew she was having too much to drink, but we were having fun. I enjoyed seeing your mother having a good time and didn't want to spoil it. We were bar hopping and had just heard of a new place to try. Since we both had our cars, we made plans to meet there.

"I'm not much of a drinker, more of a smoker, so I was fine. I wanted to offer to drive, but was afraid of agitating your mother with the suggestion. Knew it was selfish of me but, nonetheless, didn't want my own fun evening to come to an end.

"I should have put safety before my fear of your mother's reaction. That bad decision has affected so many lives."

"Hazel, my mother is strong-willed, and she wouldn't have listened to you. Stop blaming yourself. Is this why you suggested to my grandfather that you and she be neighbors?"

"Yes. Your grandfather called me up and asked for my help. I sensed he had no idea of your mother being with me that night, and felt the need to make amends." Hazel began to cry. "Kerrie, your whole presence radiates the warmth I mentioned in your smile. I love you, and am truly sorry about all the hurt you were taking in, and ashamed of not stopping her. I just stood there and let it happen." I braced myself with the door and grabbed Hazel for a hug.

"I love you too, Hazel. You interjected that helping my mother had been your idea. You attempted to defend me, but you were dismissed. Look, my mother was in a mode to rant, and nobody could stop her. Best to just let her get it all out." I stepped back, leaned against the car, and, extending my arms to reach Hazel's shoulders, looked her in the eyes. "Listen to me, Hazel, I don't blame you. You need to shed this guilt you've been carrying. Promise me you will."

"Okay, Kerrie. I will miss you. Do you have everything?"

"I'll miss you too." I looked to Kirk for the answer.

"Told Erin to get your laptop. I will come back for your clothes at another time. We needed to get out of there as quickly as possible."

"I want my pillow."

"I'll get it," said Hazel. She darted off, and I sat down in the car, but kept my door open. In no time, she returned, handed me my pillow, and backed up into the yard.

"Bye, Hazel. And do what I told you."

"I will, and have a safe trip back." I gave one last wave before we took off.

Kirk and I were in the back seat. He had his arms wrapped tightly around me, trying to keep my body still. Erin was in the front with the driver, who didn't waste time getting to the plane.

We boarded and I took a seat. Erin hung out with the pilot. Kirk went to the back and returned with a glass of bourbon. "Drink this. It will take the edge off." He held the glass to my mouth and I took small sips. When I finished the drink, my nerves had settled down, but I felt numb about what my mother had said to me. I also was numb about Erin and Kirk witnessing it. I looked out the window and zoned out. I wanted to slip back into my silent place for solace and disappear.

26

DROP OFF

Wesley picked us up at the plane. Kerrie remained quiet and hugged her pillow the whole ride to the rehabilitation center. Kirk asked me to sit with her so he could update Wesley on recent events. Kerrie was physically sitting beside me, but mentally had escaped into her own little world. I got tired of the sound of my own voice and stopped talking. Didn't believe she could even hear me in the place where she was currently residing.

"We have arrived," Kirk announced. The car pulled into a slightly inclined, gated driveway, which wrapped around to the front door. It looked more like a personal residence. Wasn't surprised, really. Kirk had referred to the facility as a top-rated luxury rehab. Wouldn't expect anything less with Kirk at the helm. Wesley let us off at the entrance.

Greeting us were our admissions counselor, Lisa, and client advocate, Alex. This would be where we parted ways. Kerrie and I were escorted to her room, while Kirk stayed back to finish the paperwork.

"Normally, I would be taking you on a tour," said Alex, "but it probably would be best to get Kerrie settled in." Alex was adorable, with a captivating, energetic personality. The youthful enthusiasm she displayed made it difficult to guess her age. "A medical assessment is to be done in a little while. One of our MDs will be determining detox requirements." Kerrie's aloofness persisted. She had on a blank stare and kept her hands tucked inside her pockets. She had handed over her pillow to me for that purpose.

"Would it be possible for me to take the tour while Kerrie is with the doctor?" I thought of the tour as a good way to get information regarding Kerrie's behavior.

"Yes. I allotted time for it in my schedule."

"Great!" We got to the room, and in a short time a couple of staff members came to get Kerrie for her evaluation. Kirk arrived as they were walking down the hallway.

"What's going on?" asked Kirk.

"Kerrie is being taken for a medical assessment for detox. You're in time for the tour." I left her pillow on a chair in the corner of the room.

"Excellent. I'm impressed with the efficiency of the staff. Made the whole admissions process painless."

"I'm pleased to hear that," Alex said. "Striving for the highest quality of personal service is of the utmost importance to us, because we understand how crucial it is to receive. And it all starts with the initial introduction to our facility. Speaking of which, let me show you around. I'll be happy to answer questions and address any concerns you may have."

"I'm glad, because I have both," I said.

"I can see you both are worried, and want to put your minds at ease. So, fire away as we walk around the grounds."

"Appreciate it, Alex," said Kirk. "I only have one question, or maybe more of a curiosity. Everybody I've met so far has been very attentive, and I'm wondering if their dedication is strictly job-related?"

"Good question, Kirk," replied Alex. "Everyone has a story, but I will answer your question by telling you mine. The struggles I battled came from a narcissistic parent, who manipulated me with different techniques and lashed out often with criticism. My response came from a desire to please. This proved to be an impossible task. Left me with a chronic feeling of never quite measuring up."

"Which parent, and how so?" I asked. "Hope you don't mind me asking, but sounds an awful lot like Kerrie's situation with her mom."

"Not at all. It was my mother, also. The similarity is why I am assigned to Kerrie. Based on my own experience, I hope to help you understand what she is going through. I work with the detox staff, as well. The set up here allows me, as a healthcare professional, to serve in an advocacy role. Have I satisfied your curiosity, Kirk?"

"Yes. I understand this is personal for you. And, knowing that, am even more impressed."

"Good. Anyway, back to the other part of your question, Erin. Judgment is based on the level of care, affection, or compliments received. Let's say I was ninety-nine percent attentive to those needs. The narcissist focuses on the one percent. This is due to a need to be in total control, and the verbal abuse is relentless."

"Yeah! Kirk and I witnessed that. Is help possible? Kerrie's mom was committed for evaluation and released."

"I read about what transpired in Kerrie's file. Thank you for calling it in. Hazel gave me a 'CliffsNotes' version of background information, as well. The medical assessment will also include diagnosis of co-occurring disorders. Underlying issues often motivate addiction. So, all information is useful.

"Concerning the release, I am not surprised. Although I can't definitively diagnose Kerrie's mom, I can say she does exhibit many of the traits of a narcissistic personality disorder. This disorder is difficult for even mental health professionals to deal with. Behaviors associated with narcissism are arrogance, entitlement, and criticism of others. These act as defense mechanisms, which mask the reality of feeling unloved and unlovable. And they're so ingrained it can be difficult to break through."

"How did you cope?"

"The same way as Kerrie. Before I explain, it might be beneficial to share the thought process. Despite the difficulty, I always felt it would be wrong to stop my attempts to satisfy my mother's needs. I bought into all her reactions being justified, which created doubt in even my slightest perception that my mother's behavior was wrong. This led to second guessing my own emotional reactions. Society dictates sticking by family, which clearly defines an expectation. So, it seemed failing to do so would be disgraceful.

"In my younger years, I thought the criticism was just normal instructional parenting. At that time, it came in the form of correcting my actions. Had no frame of reference to teach me otherwise. Found myself always on edge and believed my inability to deal with my mother was on me, not her. This was because times with my mother weren't all bad.

"There were times when I was surprised by purchases she made for me. Also, times where compliments were thrown my way. Both made me feel good but also brought shame for the hurt feelings I felt. Mostly due to my inability to get over the hurt. Began wondering if I was overreacting. I resided in a box of conflicted emotions.

"I am sorry for talking so much, but I believe my story mirrors Kerrie's to some degree. Any of this familiar to what you know about Kerrie?"

"You have touched on many characteristics Kerrie shared with me. She is very private, but I got her to open up once after some cathartic crying. The traits Kerrie shared make even more sense, but I don't understand how she is acting. It's like she is somewhere else."

"I saw what you mean. Couldn't help but notice on the way to the room. That's a way of coping, which Kerrie probably picked up in childhood."

"Kerrie did mention the comfort she found in complete darkness and silence."

"I'll now explain my way of coping, because I did the same thing. Dissociation is the technical term, which is shutting down as a means of escaping the intensity of our emotional pain. In college, I found myself overcome with anxiety and unable to focus. I began using drugs commonly known as speed, uppers, or pep pills. These are all street names for the prescription Hazel told me Kerrie was taking. It helped me focus and relieved my anxiety. I was on cloud nine and didn't want to lose this feeling, which fueled my dependency."

"How did you get better?" I asked. "With your friendly and confident disposition, I would never have guessed. I also have to say you could pass for a high school student."

"Thank you! I am twenty-six. Truth be told, I was a patient here. Upon completing my recovery, I realized I wanted to help others experiencing the same difficulties."

"Does that mean you will share your story with Kerrie?"

"My experience allows me to truly understand Kerrie, which I know is why you're asking. There is nothing I have shared with you that Kerrie doesn't already know. The productive life she has led is proof. She couldn't have moved forward without some understanding. She only needs a reminder, which will come in therapy. And after that, I might tell her. It's always nice to connect with someone who has lived through the same issues. Seeing you're not alone can provide affirmation that adds to strength.

"I can appreciate the concern you both have for her, and wanted to reassure you about Kerrie's outcome by telling my story. As you said earlier, Kirk, it's personal for me."

"I feel better already," said Kirk. "What about you, Erin?"

"Me, too. Thank you for taking the time with us, Alex. I find your candor refreshing and comforting. Is it painful to talk about? You didn't appear as if it was."

"Before becoming a patient here, I found it difficult to be open. I was also private, because of the shame I felt. Now, I view speaking out as a way of helping others. Makes the whole thing more palatable. We all want the best results for Kerrie. Your support will be even more crucial once she is released. Follow-up care will assist in sustaining her to prevent relapse. These gardens will be our last stop. I better head back to Kerrie."

"It's so peaceful," I said, "with the gardens overlooking the ocean."

"We will leave from here," added Kirk, "since Kerrie is zoned out."

"Sure. Take your time." Alex handed me her card. "If something comes to mind or you just want to chat, give me a call. One last note I want to leave you with—even with understanding, slight conflict still remains. Understanding provides you with the reality the relationship most likely won't change. The mind retains that knowledge, but the heart wishes it were different. This is why it's so easy to get cajoled back in with the smallest bit of positive attention received. I surmise this happened with Kerrie. It is not a problem, as long as all the pieces can stay intact, if the outcome turns toxic."

"On that note," Kirk said, "I must ask how to proceed pertaining to Kerrie's relationship with her mother, especially since you said it most likely won't change. The reason for me asking is I'm going back to collect the rest of Kerrie's things. I certainly don't want to encourage a relationship, which has proven to be harmful to Kerrie, but how should I respond if her mother expresses an interest in having one?"

"I appreciate your dilemma. My suggestion would be to simply assure her you will be in contact after Kerrie is home. No more needs to be said, because this is truly all you can do at this point. The success of any future relationship would be incumbent on boundaries being set and respected. The absence of which relates to the statement you quoted me on. Therapy will instruct Kerrie on this. Other than that, you have my card, and don't hesitate to call me."

"I won't, and thanks." Alex smiled sweetly and took off. Kirk and I hung out for a bit, and then did the same.

27

_____

DETOX BEGINS

I walked down the hallway to Kerrie's room. Dr. Clark, our detox physician, was coming toward me. "Alex, I'm glad you're back. I was hoping to catch you. Heard you are assigned to Kerrie's case."

"Yes. Did everything go all right? Got Jana to cover for me so I could reassure Kerrie's friends."

"I know. Jana is doing a good job with her. How did Kerrie seem to you?"

"Withdrawn, which is not surprising considering the verbal attack she received moments before her arrival."

"Did you get any additional information from Kerrie's friends?"

"They confirmed what I thought to be true based on my own experience. Hazel, a friend of her mom, gave me the name of the medication that was taken. She is also a nurse and was helpful in relaying the symptoms witnessed."

"I read all that, but wanted to get your opinion of her. What confirmation did you get?"

"What is with all the questions, Tom? Is Kerrie okay, and how did the evaluation go? I need to know what happened to help me with how to answer."

"Fair enough. Kerrie was quiet and jittery. Hands kept shaking, and Jana had to hold her still so Tyler could get vitals and draw blood."

"Yeah. I did notice she kept them deep inside her pockets. Being jittery and tremors are symptoms Hazel clued me in on. Were you able to get her talking?"

"Only short answers. Anyway, probably would not be a stretch to presume Kerrie suffers from an anxiety disorder linked to family dysfunction."

"I agree. I must say you have an eloquent way of stating the obvious. Just saying. So, what do you need my opinion on? I presume you prescribed medication for the anxiety to calm her down and induce sleep."

"I gave you that one and, yes, that was the plan. I spoke with Kerrie about treating the anxiety. She didn't refuse until I mentioned medicating her with a sedative, at which point she freaked and raced to the bathroom. She won't be able to keep anything down in this condition. Do you have any ideas about what may have caused her reaction?"

"I have a few, but only one is most likely the cause. You probably should have started by telling me what happened."

"Probably so, but I wanted to see if you had any behavioral insight that would give me the explanation I was looking for, without having to rehash. I'm sure it was like asking you for a needle in a haystack."

"A bit like that. It's hard to give a single answer to such a broad topic without a specific question. I will consult with Nia about holistic alternatives. How is Kerrie now?"

"She seemed to settle down after I dropped the sedative plan. Jana brought her back to the room and I came looking for you. Never did tell me your idea about the cause."

"Right. Hazel had given Kerrie's mother a sedative to calm her down, after all the ranting. She mentioned this to Kerrie in their last conversation, which took place right before Kerrie got in the car to leave. As I told her friend, Erin, Kerrie uses dissociation to escape the intensity of emotional pain. More specifically, during this matter, she shut down to separate from the memory of the incident and all associated feelings erupting inside."

"So, when I made my sedative suggestion?"

"Kerrie was immediately brought back to the recent trauma. The origin of the intense emotional pain I referenced earlier dates back to her childhood. I never considered the possibility of the treatment plan being a trigger. Let me go see what I can do to help."

"I didn't know about her mom, but I'm not sure it would have made a difference for me, either. I'll head back to my office. I'm glad I caught you."

"Me, too. Thanks, Tom."

I entered a dark room. Jana blocked my view of Kerrie, who was sitting on the floor in a corner. In this business, nothing was odd, because unusual behavior was a norm with drug withdrawal. I assumed Jana was still trying to console Kerrie. Tom did speak of her doing a good job with Kerrie. "How's it going?" Jana quickly turned around.

"Alex, thank goodness you're here. I can't reach her. She told me about having a headache and—"

"Slow down, Jana. Your rapid speech is giving *me* a headache." I walked over to assess the problem and found Kerrie in a catatonic stupor.

"How long has she been like this?"

"Not long. Maybe five to ten minutes. And I'm sorry about bombarding you with information."

"You're fine. I understand how scary this is." Kerrie was sitting with her back against the wall, legs stretched out, and head down, hugging her pillow. "Kerrie, can you hear me? I need you to look me in the eyes." No response, which was what I expected.

"Okay, Jana. Kerrie actually told you about having a headache?"

"Yes, and asked me to turn off all the lights. She moved the chair away from the corner and grabbed her pillow. I saw expression leave her eyes as she slid down the wall. She's been immobile and muted ever since. Did Dr. Clark find you?"

"He did. I need you to page him." Jana went into the hallway while I continued trying to get Kerrie to respond.

"I'm here, Alex," Dr. Clark said, walking into the room. "Are you having any luck?"

"That was quick. No luck whatsoever." I never turned away from Kerrie. "My first impression is the only explanation, and I wanted to be wrong."

"I was close by, checking on another patient. I know what you mean. Catatonia is something you can never get used to seeing."

"True. Told Jana I understood how scary this is, because she was unnerved."

"Still am," said Jana. "Don't think I'll ever get the image out of my head. What do you need me to get?"

"Let's give her Lorazepam," said Dr. Clark. "It will also help with the anxiety, tremors, and insomnia. Hopefully, we can have her sleep through the detoxification. If not, at least it will help with the withdrawal symptoms. My initial plan is working out, after all. I just wish it wasn't under these circumstances. I'll go put the order in the computer. Keep me posted."

"Okay." I stayed with Kerrie while Jana left to get the Lorazepam. Watched Kerrie the whole time I was speaking with Tom. She never moved, and her gaze remained fixed on the floor. One look into Kerrie's eyes reminded me of my own suffering. The lack of expression portrayed a lost soul that could not find its way out. I wanted to be able to help her, but all I could do was anxiously await Jana's return. In my concerned state, her return seemed to be taking a painfully long while, but looking at my phone told me not much time had passed.

"I got it," Jana cried out. Relief immediately replaced my concern. Jana approached with a tray of everything needed. I injected medication into Kerrie's arm, and soon she slipped into the Land of Nod.

"Before we put her to bed, let's change these clothes. We will replace them with a gown, in case her body temp spikes." Jana grabbed a new one from the supply cabinet and removed the plastic wrap. She had only been with us a few weeks but was a fast learner.

"That makes sense. Kerrie's temp has been normal, but that doesn't mean it won't change, since excessive sweating is a known symptom."

"Correct. Take from what you know and prepare for it all." We teamed up to carefully maneuver Kerrie's body so we could change her clothes and put her to bed without disrupting her sleep. When we managed to get it done, we both breathed a sigh of relief. "Thank you for all your help, Jana. I can take it from here. Go home."

"Are you sure?"

"Yes. Catch some Z's. Looks like you can use it."

"I am tired, so I'm not going to ask twice. See you tomorrow, Alex." She took off before I had a chance to respond. I sat down and settled in for a long night.

28

A MUCH NEEDED REST

It was comforting to see Kerrie resting. Lying there peacefully, her face revealed a sweet personality. We were strongly recommended against getting attached to patients. I had never understood how you could effectively distance yourself from the care you gave. Although, some patients made it very easy for you not to form attachments. Kerrie certainly wasn't one of those patients. Had an inkling, from reading her file, that she might be different.

Before Kerrie arrived, Lisa had quietly handed me her file, which had a comment attached. The sticky note informed me that I had been assigned this case, and told me to read the information in the folder ASAP to find out why. The sticky note had done its job—my curiosity had been piqued. I proceeded to the parlor, sat down in a recliner, and opened the folder.

The left flap contained contact information and had a highlighted note clipped on top that made it clear I should contact Helen for clinical details. The right flap contained the patient information that Kirk had called in prior to getting Kerrie. The only information known at that time had been a stimulant addiction. An update added later spoke of the recent incident between Kerrie and her mother. This reading was plenty for me to paint a picture of Kerrie's life. I could relate to her experience, and knew why I had been chosen to be her counselor.

Lisa paged me up front when their car arrived at the gate. It was then I understood the reason for the ASAP. I had recently ended a call with Hazel and had just finished adding a few notes of my own to the file. Hazel had provided me with some background information, which validated my picture. With the folder in hand, I rose from the chair. I reached Lisa in time to see the car drive up.

I suggested to Lisa we move to greet them. I explained that standing stationary, waiting for them to come to us, made me feel like I should be welcoming them to "Fantasy Island." The show was before my time, but I loved to catch episodes on Nostalgia, a local station that strictly played TV series from the late seventies and early eighties. It was great for winding down after my shift was over.

Kirk exited the car first. Erin got out next, and came around to help with Kerrie. Kirk opened the door, and Erin leaned in to talk to her. It was easy to see their close friendship. Erin backed up and Kerrie got out. She passed her pillow to Erin. Her pockets instantly became a hiding spot for her hands.

Kerrie's sadness and composure tugged at my heartstrings. That is, after I got over my shock at her emaciated condition. My inkling of Kerrie being different was correct, because we ordinarily got clients who exhibited extreme irritability. I got the distinct impression that being placid was Kerrie's go-to nature, which I attributed to all the distress caused her from a confrontational environment.

In my recovery, I had realized an opportunity to reinvent myself, which had coincided with a new understanding. Tired of being uptight and miserable, I strove to be happy. I became determined to make a difference with the insight I had gained. It stood to reason that writing allowed Kerrie to do the same.

I noticed Kerrie begin to stir and grimace, which summoned me bedside. Thought she might be in pain. While I stood there monitoring her, her stirs became more like shivers and she suddenly sat up in fright. Kerrie opened her mouth as if to scream, but nothing came out. I grabbed a hand and got her attention.

"Kerrie, you must have had a nightmare. I'm Alex and am in charge of your care." She looked around the room, trying to orient herself. "Do you remember me?" Kerrie's attention returned to me, and she appeared to become cognizant of her surroundings.

"You brought me and Erin to my room."

"Yes. Are you better now?"

"I'm still rattled from the nightmare. It was so realistic. How long have you been here?"

"The whole time you've been sleeping." I caught a glimpse of a shadow in the doorway. I turned and saw it was Tyler.

"Is this a bad time?" asked Tyler.

"No. Come on in." Kerrie looked troubled.

"Are you leaving, Alex?"

"I'm not going anywhere. This is Tyler. He took blood from you earlier and checked your vitals."

"Now I'm back to do the same."

"Right. I remember you now. My mind is a bit foggy."

"Understand. I can see you're tired. Stop fighting to keep your eyes open." Kerrie quietly watched until Tyler finished, and then gave in.

"Thanks, Tyler."

"Sure thing, Alex. Call if you need me." Tyler scooted out the door. We had worked together for quite some time, becoming fast friends, and made a good team.

With Kerrie back to sleep, I moved the chair closer. I searched the room for reading material before sitting down. It was a known fact around the center that I was frequently in search of a good book. I often asked my coworkers what they'd been reading lately.

Now the staff had taken to leaving their book recommendations for me in different rooms. Looking around, I saw only one book, its cover hidden by a note. The note was from Lisa, who had written that she thought I might find it interesting. I lifted the paper and unveiled Kerrie's book, *Misguided*. I was happy to have it. Reading it could possibly help me know her better. I sat down and began to read.

29

HELLO MORNING

I read through the night, with only a brief interruption from Tyler. He called to check in with me. The book had been an easy read, and I was about a chapter shy of finishing. I needed to stand up and stretch. The sun lit up the room, so I moved to the window to close the blinds, and returned to the bed. Kerrie's leg raised and dropped. The impact caused Kerrie to sit up again in fear. I sat down on the edge of the bed.

"Let me guess. You had a dream about falling."

"Yeah. How did you know?"

"I've had those a few times myself, and awaken when my leg thumps the bed. Lie back down and get more rest." Kerrie started stretching and rubbing her arms and legs. "Tell me what is wrong."

"I ache all over. And I'd rather not sleep anymore, if I'm going to continue to have nightmares. Alex, can you give me something to help me stay awake?"

"Kerrie, you know the answer, considering that's why you're here. I can medicate to make you more comfortable, though."

"Right. I wasn't thinking, because my mind was focused on avoiding nightmares. Will the medication put me to sleep?"

"Yes, but the rest is necessary in order to give your body a chance to build strength and get past this stage. Sleep deprivation exacerbates the withdrawal."

"Okay, Alex." Kerrie's sleepy eyes resembled the puffy eyes stoners get. She spoke in a whisper, and tremors returned to her hands. "I need to go to the bathroom."

"Scoot to the edge, take my hand, and stand up slow." The combination of weakness from lack of sleep, pain, and tremors caused her to walk carefully. "I need you to leave me a sample." Wanted to get an updated report on drug levels. "Containers are in the above cabinet. I will give you privacy, but call me when you're finished." Kerrie nodded in compliance. I was astonished that she didn't complain. By now, other clients would have been exhibiting mood swings or become crazed with cravings. She quietly endured the suffering her body language clearly expressed.

Staying outside the door, I kept it cracked so I could hear if any problems cropped up. The bathroom was elaborate, like in a fancy hotel or resort. It included a double vanity, step-up marble Jacuzzi, and separate tile shower. Even with the door open, there was still plenty of privacy. While waiting, I called Tyler to pick up the sample. My ulterior motive was that I wanted him to assist with the injection, which I came clean with him about.

Heard the sink faucet running longer than necessary and rushed in. I discovered Kerrie sitting across from the sink with her eyes closed, struggling to get control of her shaky hands to rub her right temple.

"Kerrie, open your eyes."

"I can't. My head is throbbing and the lights are too bright."

"What's going on?" asked Tyler, stepping into the bathroom.

"Kerrie has a headache. Can you shut off the lights?"

"Yeah, but why is the faucet running?"

"Oh, yeah. She probably was washing her hands and, with her head hurting, sat down and forgot to shut it off. Seeing Kerrie like this, it slipped my mind, also." Tyler turned the faucet off and flipped the switch.

"I am going to drop off this sample, since you're not ready for my help yet."

"Good idea, but hurry back."

"I will."

"Kerrie, the lights are off. I need you to open your eyes." Keeping her fingers in place, she slowly opened her eyes. "Are you aware you left the faucet on?" I could see Kerrie trying to comprehend the question.

"Faucet?" If I didn't already know from the delay, this noticeable confusion confirmed a definite cognitive impairment.

"Let me get you back to bed, and then we can take care of your headache." Kerrie's fingers remained pressed into her forehead.

"Four aspirin. It takes four aspirin to relieve my headaches." Her response was again delayed, but she made the request clearly. The clarity, no doubt, related to the relief she had mentioned. As I helped Kerrie up, Tyler walked in.

"You didn't get far," said Tyler. "Thought you'd have her in bed by now."

"She is having difficulty concentrating. I asked her if she remembered leaving the faucet on and her eyes glazed over. Help me get her to bed."

"Why don't I take over and you get the medication?"

"That's a better idea." I prepared the syringe and returned to Kerrie. She kept her head perfectly still, which must have been difficult given her physical discomfort.

"Do you have the aspirin for my headache?"

"I have something else that will help." Tyler held her arm. That was why I'd needed him. Giving injections could be unnerving on its own, but with tremors or possible sudden movements added to the mix, you needed a backup. As she had before, Kerrie soon slipped off to sleep.

"Hey, guys," said Jana. "I finally made it."

"I wondered if you were coming in. After yesterday's drama, I thought maybe you needed a day."

"Tyler!" Jana yelled.

"Oops. Sorry, Jana. I forgot, but I'll tell Alex now."

"Tell me what?" I asked.

"I passed Jana in the hall earlier, and she gave me a message for you." Tyler cleared his throat. "Jana was called to cover for another case, but will be here as soon as she can get away." Jana did not look amused.

"Cute, Tyler. I'm here now, so I could have told her."

"No. It was my task to pass the message on, and now I have." Jana managed to crack a smile, and then they both busted out laughing. They were always ribbing each other. "My work here is done, so I'm heading out."

"See you later, Tyler."

"Yes, you will, or I'll have Jana give you a message."

"I have no witty response," sighed Jana. "Hate when that happens." I knew what she meant. Happened to me with Tom, sometimes. It was frustrating.

"What can I do for you, Alex?" Jana said.

"I believe we are good." I picked up the book and sat down. "I'm going to finish my reading."

"That's a really good book. I read it when it first came out."

"Lisa left it for me. Thought I might find it interesting, because of the author."

"Seriously? I could see recommending the book for the story. Don't get me wrong, I think authors are amazing, but it's the story that hooks you. Unless you're interested in a specific genre—then I can see an author recommendation. Is that it?"

"You are turning this into a mystery, and it's really not. The answer is sleeping." Jana squinted her eyes, looking puzzled and trying to make sense of what I'd said. Suddenly, her eyes lit up. She scanned the book's cover.

"Oh my gosh! Our patient is Kerrie Brannon. I don't retain last names, so I didn't make the connection."

"You are correct. Thought I might be able to find out Kerrie's personality by reading her book."

"That makes total sense. I don't want to say anything that could be a spoiler, so I'll quietly hang out and let you finish. I'm actually due for a break, but I've been running around all morning, and would rather stay put. I brought some magazines to go through. Okay, shutting up now." Jana sat down on the sofa and spread her magazines across the coffee table.

"I understand. It'll be nice to have the company."

"I'm sure you're tired. Why don't you lie down and read yourself to sleep? I've got this." I was beginning to feel sleepy, and the thought of taking a nap appealed to me.

"I'll take you up on your offer, since my eyes are feeling heavy. And that makes for a strong probability of me falling asleep once I begin reading. I should warn you, though, that Kerrie's been having disturbing dreams and waking up startled. But she settles down easily when you talk to her."

"Noted. Sounds easy enough. Although, I was beginning to get concerned by your initial phrasing. Especially after yesterday's situation. Get some rest."

"Thanks, and sorry about that. I wasn't thinking. Further confirmation of needing sleep." Jana agreed, picked up a magazine, and buried herself inside.

When assigned to a case, you were responsible for around-the-clock care. The room had a second bed for that reason. Our detox team provided support by keeping watch. During your sleep, another member stayed inside the room to be readily available, which I liked. With Jana here, I could allow myself to fall into a sound sleep. I was generally a light sleeper, but wouldn't want to rely on that if Kerrie were to wake up.

Kerrie was my first patient. I thought of my job as being assigned to be Kerrie's roommate during her stay here. Or at least through detox. The purpose was to create a reassuring familiarity for the client. It was another way to provide comfort and nurture healing. Making no pretense at reading, I closed my eyes.

30

FEELING REFRESHED

Slept as much as I could and woke up. Jana was flipping through another magazine. She had settled into the sofa by stretching her legs out. I sat up and caught Jana's attention.

"Welcome back. You must feel better."

"I do, actually. Can't sleep any more. Everything go all right?"

"Yeah. Kerrie woke up startled, like you said. I spoke to her, and she asked for you. I pointed out that you were asleep in the next bed. After catching a glimpse, she slipped back to sleep."

"Are you okay to hang out for a bit longer? I'd like to hop in the shower."

"Absolutely. Kerrie is different and a refreshing change from some patient types."

"I had that very same thought." I opened up one of the drawers to get a change of clothes. Housekeeping kept them well stocked, with an assortment of scrubs. They were comfortable and doubled as sleepwear.

The shower felt good. An idea popped into my head. I decided to follow up on an earlier suggestion. I exited the bathroom to find my phone. Looked around the room in the usual places.

"No change, Alex." Jana addressed the question she knew I'd eventually get around to asking. "You look better. Not that you looked bad before."

"Relax. I know what you mean." I interrupted Jana, to save her from continuing to explain herself. "Did you happen to see my phone?"

"I have it. Your phone buzzed and I grabbed it, in case any of our staff were trying to reach you." Jana handed me my phone and I sat down next to her, placing it on the side table.

"Thanks. And?"

"And what?"

"Was it staff?"

"Oh. Sorry. No, it wasn't. Kind of figured it wouldn't be, since they generally just drop in, but wanted to be safe."

"I can appreciate that. Only asked because I was curious. I'm going to contact Nia about aromatherapy."

"Ooh, aromatherapy is awesome. I could do with a whiff of peppermint myself. Beginning to feel my energy fading with all this non-activity."

"I hear ya. Why don't you take off? Your shift is about over anyway."

"Actually, I picked up a second shift, so I'll go to my room and get some rest before it starts." There were a dozen of us who worked, with minimal time between shifts. We each had a room on the second floor. It didn't make sense to waste time driving home when we could stay and sleep. The estate had a limit of six clients. One team member was assigned to each, and the remaining members were floaters.

"I will probably see you later, then."

"Count on it." I was about to call Nia, when her voice drifted in from the doorway. It was crazy when that happened, as if communication were occurring through osmosis.

"Hey, Nia. I literally was just about to call you."

"We must be on the same wavelength. I saw Tom this morning, and he filled me in on Kerrie. He explained you mentioned talking to me, but then you had a situation. I have a break in my schedule, so I thought I'd stop by and see if you are ready for my help."

"I am. I administered a second dose of Lorazepam, which is why Kerrie is sleeping. Prior to that, she was experiencing recurring tremors, joined by muscle aches and pains. She also complained of a throbbing headache, and her eyes were closed and she was rubbing her right temple. Jana had a similar experience with Kerrie having a headache prior to the situation you mentioned."

"Sounds like a migraine. Does Kerrie have a history?"

"She intimated as much by telling me it takes four aspirin to get relief."

"Yes, would be a safe assumption. How about alertness?"

"Limited, and I noticed trouble thinking. Hard to pinpoint whether all these symptoms have separate causes, or are withdrawal related. Whatever the reason, I want treatment switched to a natural remedy source."

"I can appreciate the difficulty in knowing for sure, but we have a number of essential oils available. Each one has its own healing properties, regardless of the cause. I can start setting up, if you like."

"Nia, you have gotten to the heart of what I want. Ideally, I'd like everything ready when Kerrie wakes up."

"I aim to please, Alex. Your request is definitely doable. Kerrie doesn't appear to be ready to wake up any time soon."

"I'm hoping and anticipating she'll sleep through the night. If we set up this evening, we'll be able to begin when she wakes in the morning."

"I get it. This is a way of preventing the prep time from causing a delay in treatment. I'll go gather what I need and be right back." Nia hurried off, and I reclaimed my bedside chair. Kerrie was in a deep sleep, and with the silence, I picked up

Misguided. Being close to the end, I felt confident I could complete the book before Nia returned.

31

PREPARATION

Nia set up the massage table in the corner. She left the sheet set neatly folded on top and moved on to her aromatherapy products. I had finished the book with time to spare. Kerrie had tossed and turned a few times, but remained asleep. Even if she had wanted to wake up, exhaustion controlled her. Fatigue generally took over when the effects of the medication wore off, and kept the slumber going.

"My plan is to start with a bath and move onto the massage later, which is why I'm making bath salts," Nia explained. She was busy sorting through her case, a crafted wooden box with a painted lighthouse scene on its lid. It opened up to inserts of different shapes and sizes used to store and display essential oils. A bowl was on the counter, along with a glass jar.

"I've read about bath salts being used as a way of safely adding essential oils to a bath."

"Far better to learn through reading than the hard way. In this case, it would be by burning your skin. Since oil and water don't mix, this could potentially happen. Essential oils disperse in a bath when mixed with salt."

"Could not agree more. What ingredients are you using?"

"Dead Sea salt with drops of eucalyptus, lavender, and peppermint. Each one offers relief from the symptoms we discussed."

"Jana mentioned earlier how she could use a whiff of peppermint. She felt her energy fading."

"Peppermint is known to put pep back in your step. It's a natural energy booster. Both peppermint and eucalyptus enhance mental alertness and concentration. Eucalyptus also helps with migraines and muscle aches and pains. Lavender is commonly used for calming, which can be beneficial in countering Kerrie's anxiety disorder, but it heals migraines, as well. When I was setting up the massage table, I noticed a pillow in the corner."

"Kerrie likes having her own pillow. She was sitting in that very corner hugging it when I first sedated her. I'd forgotten it was even there."

"Looked like the pillow came from home, based on its silk pillowcase. I hoped it belonged to her. I don't imagine Kerrie has thought about it much, either, with her fog of fatigue and other issues."

"She hasn't asked for it, but most likely will once the effects of the aromatherapy kick in. Why were you hoping?"

"Another of lavender's therapeutic properties is sedation. We can add a few drops to her pillow before bedtime to ensure a good night's sleep, without the nightmares associated with anxiety."

"Wow, Nia. I haven't even told you about Kerrie having nightmares."

"I'm not surprised. The combination of her existing anxiety with that caused by withdrawal compounds her symptoms.

Nightmares are one, and insomnia can be another." Nia finished mixing the ingredients in the bowl and poured the contents into a jar. After tightening the lid, she shook the jar several times. "Believe we are all set. I'll be back early in the morning so I can hopefully get here before Kerrie wakes."

"I like that plan. It will give us a chance to discuss how to proceed. See you bright and early."

"Yes to both." Jana entered as Nia was leaving. "Hello, Jana. Heard you were in need of some peppermint earlier."

"That I was, Nia. I've taken a nap since, so I'm good to go, but if you're offering me some, I won't turn it down."

"I wasn't, but I give you credit for the suggestion. If you are truly interested, however, I might be able to hook you up."

"Awesome! I am definitely interested."

"Okay. I imagine we'll be running into each other again, so we can talk then."

"For sure, particularly since you'll be working with Kerrie. Are you heading home?"

"Yes, but will be back early. See ya."

"So long, and thanks."

32

AROMATHERAPY

Nia arrived early, as she promised, complete with case in hand and scheduling book tucked under her arm. She sat her book down and slipped into our bathroom to set the case on the vanity. I was ready for our discussion, because I had again enlisted Jana to cover for me while I slept. Even instructed her to be my morning alarm, because I wanted a bite of breakfast and, more importantly, coffee before we got started. All my preparation had done the trick, and I was raring to go.

Before Jana got called away, she gave me an uneventful report, in which Kerrie did nothing more than sleep. No surprise there, because excessive sleep typically occurred after a patient stopped taking stimulants. In fact, it was not unheard of for a patient to sleep sixteen to twenty hours at a time. Kerrie was still sleeping heavily, nearing the twenty-hour mark. This boded well for our aromatherapy plans. I positioned myself on the sofa to supervise her, and noticed Nia quietly coming toward me. I patted the sofa for her to sit beside me.

"With the long hours Kerrie has been sleeping, our timing for aromatherapy is perfect," I said. "I totally defer to your expertise, but want to begin by discussing my role as far as bridging the gap between her waking and bathing. We touched upon the nightmares responsible for jolting Kerrie awake, and I expect this morning will be no different."

"Speaking to your initial comment," Nia said, "the length of sleep definitely is advantageous. I can appreciate your anxiousness regarding the horror that nightmares produce, and your associated motivation to have interim treatment measures established. I suggest we start by having Kerrie drink as much water as she can handle and follow up with her taking a shower. I will prepare the bath while she is in the shower."

"Thanks for your suggestion, Nia. I always like knowing what I'm doing before an emergency strikes, which could possibly hinder my ability to think."

"Duly noted. The Dead Sea salt will assist in eliminating toxins, so we'll continue her water consumption during and after the bath to prevent dehydration." Mindful that Kerrie would wake soon, I remained focused on her while still managing to take in everything Nia was saying. "We can schedule massages as needed, using appropriate essential oils, to ensure Kerrie's comfort." I jumped up at the sight of Kerrie stirring and the sound of her murmuring. Standing beside her, I could see eyelids flickering. I wondered if this meant she was getting closer to waking up. I got my answer when Kerrie suddenly woke up, terrified.

"Alex!"

"What is it, Kerrie?"

"I need to stay awake." Kerrie spoke in a low, quivering voice. I turned my attention to Nia, and Kerrie followed my gaze.

"Kerrie, this is Nia. While you were sleeping, we made plans to start you on aromatherapy. I'll let her explain further, but I need you to drink some water as you're listening. Okay?" I couldn't determine whether her shakes were side effects of her nightmare, withdrawal, or both.

"Okay, Alex," Kerrie responded. She remained fixated on Nia and continued to shake. From this behavior, I could easily see her symptoms were strictly related to withdrawal. I seized the opportunity to get water, and Nia took my place beside her.

"Hey, Kerrie, I'll be brief, because I can see you're uncomfortable." I returned with the water, and Kerrie drank it as I had asked. "In short, essential oils can be used to relieve all your withdrawal symptoms. Even nightmares can be gotten rid of with the use of lavender prior to bedtime. I hope this calms your worry about sleep."

"Definitely willing to give it a try."

"Great! Do you have any questions or concerns?"

"Nothing like that. I'm only curious as to how you came to decide on aromatherapy, because I know acupuncture is predominantly offered in rehab."

"Well, to be perfectly honest, I have a needle phobia, and made a choice to specialize in aromatherapy over acupuncture."

"I like your answer, Nia, and am grateful you don't administer a therapy you're timid about."

"Could you imagine? It would make a good comedy skit, but dreadful reality. On that note, keep drinking, and I'll leave Alex to explain the rest." Nia got up and stepped aside as I added more water to Kerrie's cup.

"Drink up."

"I need to use the bathroom first." Kerrie didn't even wait for a response before sliding off the bed.

"You do appear stronger from all your rest but, still, take it slow and easy." I was encouraged by her ability to move more easily. "And leave a sample." After Kerrie returned, I checked that she hadn't forgotten to leave a sample and put in a request for pick-up. I was glad to see Tyler when he showed up. For some reason, I hadn't thought he'd be back. He left after picking up the sample.

I made sure Kerrie was settled before diving into my explanation.

"Our plan is for you to have an aromatherapy bath. One benefit is the removal of toxins, so I'm having you drink water to prevent dehydration. Why don't you start off in the shower while Nia prepares your bath? You can find the soap and shampoo on the vanity."

Kerrie took one last sip and headed to the bathroom. Nia waited outside to give her privacy but entered when she heard the shower door shut, and started the process. I stood in the doorway and watched as she filled the tub.

"Is everything okay, Alex?"

"Sure, just watching and pondering the concept of aromatherapy. Being a fan of candles, I find the healing aspect of scents fascinating."

"Obviously I do, too. Keeping the healing aspect in mind, I'll explain what I'm doing. I filled the tub before adding the bath salts to prevent the aroma from dissipating too quickly. Now that the tub is filled to where I want it, I'm pouring in about one cup and will stir the salts around, making sure they dissolve, of course, but also releasing the fragrances into the steam.

"Regarding your fascination, we don't have enough time for me to spout off my whole dissertation, but I will give you a snippet to think about. We don't often think about our five senses, yet we intuitively function daily from the input our mind receives from them. Nourishing smells awaken our sensibilities, triggering a healing response."

"Wow, that is so true how we often respond subconsciously."

"Yes. We're ready." Nia stepped out of the bathroom, and I knocked on the shower door.

"Kerrie, your bath is ready."

"Okay, can you get me a towel?" I placed the towel over the door. She stepped out with it wrapped around her. Using a second towel, she covered up her hair.

"I'll go grab some more water and have Nia bring it in to you. That way she can give you more information on the essential oils being used."

"Great! I am so over the shakes and pain. Nia did say they'd relieve all my withdrawal symptoms, and I'm curious to hear more about the process." She stepped up to the Jacuzzi, and I made my exit. Nia was on the sofa reading Kerrie's book. I filled her cup.

"Hey Nia, interesting reading?"

"I actually saw the movie. I knew a book had come first, but I had no idea the author was our client. Are you ready for me yet?"

"You're not the lone ranger. Jana didn't make the connection, either, and she read the book. Kerrie stepped up to the Jacuzzi before I came out here. Can you give her this water? I kinda told her you would." Nia chuckled. We'd made a joke out of the nonsensical phrase "kind of."

"I kinda better, then." Nia handed Kerrie the water, and I returned to the doorway. Kerrie must have been thirsty, because she was drinking more deeply than she had earlier.

"So, Kerrie, how are you feeling?" asked Nia.

"Great right now. I could just stay in here. What am I smelling, because obviously it has something to do with how relaxed I feel?"

"That would be the lavender. Calming properties have long been attributed to lavender. I blended it with eucalyptus, peppermint, and Dead Sea salt. I'll spare you the long description of these essential oils, because I'm sure you're more interested in their benefits to you."

"Well, I am curious to hear about the relief you mentioned earlier."

"I was speaking specifically about the symptoms Alex filled me in on. She mentioned muscle aches and pains, but also described the headaches you were having. It sounded more like migraines to me, and Alex got the impression you might have a history of having them."

"Yeah. I generally try and prevent them by taking four aspirin, if available, at the first twinge. If I don't, the pain becomes sharper above my right eye. And then I become nauseated." Kerrie continued to drink during their conversation.

"Definitely a migraine, all right. Okay, so eucalyptus helps with muscle aches and pains, but also fights migraines. Peppermint energizes, combating fatigue. I also understand you've been a little foggy, which is common during detox, and where peppermint combined with eucalyptus comes to the rescue by enhancing mental alertness and concentration. The shakes will naturally disappear, as well, when health is restored to both your mind and body. That's aromatherapy in a nutshell. Any questions?"

"No, I'm good."

"I will leave you, then, to enjoy your bath, but will be back to check on you and schedule in some massages. I was going to schedule them before leaving today, but it's probably best to take it one step at a time. Anyway, if any questions do crop up, feel free to ask them when I return or have Alex get me. Either way is fine with me." Nia grabbed her case and motioned for me to follow her.

"I wanted to inform you that I left a bottle of lavender in the drawer under the sink for her pillow like we discussed."

"Right. I'm curious as to when she'll remember it."

"Probably won't be long. The nightmare jolted her awake, plus she'll be feeling better. See ya. Call me if you need anything."

"You know I will." Nia picked up her scheduling book and disappeared down the hall. Before returning to Kerrie, I got the pitcher to refill her cup. If Kerrie hadn't been so adamant about staying awake, I would have been surprised to see her eyes open in her relaxed state.

"Are you still doing all right?" I poured her more water, and she took a few more sips.

"Yeah, I'm thirsty, but I remember you telling me the bath will remove toxins."

"Yeah, this generally occurs in the first twenty minutes. Any additional time allows you to absorb the minerals in the water from the bath salts. I think it's time for you to get out, but let me first grab you some scrubs to change into. I want to be here to help in case you begin to feel lightheaded."

"Okay. I should probably eat something." Before responding, I went and got the scrubs.

"I had the very same thought. Our chefs are top-notch." I laid the scrubs on a shelf beside the tub. "We'll finish up here and head to the dining area." I saw Kerrie immediately tense up.

"Would it be possible to eat in here? I'm not up to being around anyone else."

"What if we eat outside and take in the view?"

"I'd like that." I opened up a towel. As Kerrie carefully got out, I wrapped it around her.

"Do you have any allergies, or are there any foods you don't like?"

"No allergies, and I'm not picky."

"All right then, get dressed and I'll make the arrangements."

"Okay, I won't be long, because after hearing your rave reviews, I'm hungry."

"That makes two of us." I picked up my phone and rang down to Curtis, one of our chefs, about being served outside. He was accommodating, and enjoyed the challenge of creating special dishes for a first meal. I had just hung up the phone when Kerrie came out of the bathroom.

"You look refreshed. How do you like the scrubs?"

"I love how soft they are."

"Me, too. I believe housekeeping doubles up on the softener. Spoke with the chef and set everything up, so let's go ahead and claim our table."

"Sounds good. Can we walk the grounds after?"

"Don't see why not. You keep beating me to my suggestions, but that's okay. Suggest away." It was nice to finally get a smile out of Kerrie. We cut through the dining room to the outside stone balcony and had a seat. We were enjoying the ocean breeze when the double doors opened up, and Curtis stepped out.

"Curtis, I hope this means you'll be waiting on us personally," I gleefully said.

"It does, Alex. You are the only ones left to be fed. Hello, Kerrie. I wanted to go over my menu with you. If it is not to your liking, I'd be happy to fix you something else. Alex, on the other hand, will just have to fucking deal with it." Curtis got a laugh from us both. He not only was an awesome cook, but also always knew how to deliver a line that served up spontaneous laughter.

"You see, Kerrie, Curtis likes to mess with me because of my quirky way of ordering."

"That, and the fact she always follows up with her special brand of reasoning, which she conveniently left out."

"I'll concede that point." I could tell Kerrie was amused. "And Kerrie, I knew Curtis would like the challenge of creating a special meal for you, because, as a chef, that is what he enjoys most."

"Oh! That's why you asked me about allergies and preferences."

"Yes. So, Curtis, what delectable meal is planned for us today?"

"To start, I have prepared a tomato soup. The tomatoes are fresh from our garden. Next is a delicately prepared chicken breast with mushroom cream sauce. And for dessert is chocolate mousse. Kerrie, will that be all right with you?"

"Yes, Curtis, completely all right.

"What about you, Alex?"

"I agree with Kerrie, but…"

"Here we go."

"No, it all sounds delicious, but I was going to ask to have the chocolate mousse first. That way, I won't be too full to enjoy it."

"See what I mean, Kerrie?" Curtis quickly smirked before excusing himself, and Kerrie and I got back to enjoying the ocean breeze.

33

SEASIDE SILENCE

Kerrie ate the whole meal. I contained my delight, not wanting to make a big deal of it. Afterward, as planned, we walked the grounds, but without any conversation. Stopping at the water's edge, I watched as Kerrie looked out over the ocean. It was obvious her mind had drifted off to a distant place. Similar to when she first arrived, but different somehow. I couldn't help but wonder what she was thinking about so deeply.

More to the point, I considered whether her thoughts were pleasing or troubling, and what she was trying to work out for herself. I had drawn on my own experience to come up with those options but, considering there could be more, decided to give it a rest. Thankfully, Kerrie turned to head back. I didn't want to interrupt her but also didn't want to miss Nia, because I wanted to schedule massages before she left for the day.

I needn't have worried. Nia was sitting in the room, waiting for us with her scheduling book open on her lap. "Hey, Nia. Have you been waiting long?"

"No. I was doing paperwork, and from my window caught a glimpse of you two down at the beach. I was in need of a break, so I came to the room."

"Glad you did. I wasn't sure how long you planned on working today, and was afraid we might miss each other."

"I've got plenty of paperwork to catch up on, so will not be leaving any time soon. Regardless, I would not have left without checking back first."

"I'm relieved to know that. I noticed you reviewing your schedule. Do you have any time in mind?"

"Yes. I marked the spots. Kerrie, are you still feeling relief from your bath?"

"The only thing I'm finding bothersome is my energy dwindling."

"Along with feeling tired, are your muscles aching?"

"Yeah, but nothing I can't handle."

"In that case, I can make time to give you a massage now and knock both problems out. The thing is, you don't have to tolerate any discomfort, because we can help."

"I appreciate what you're saying. If you're sure it's no trouble, I would love a massage. I'm tired of being tired."

"No trouble whatsoever. If you're one of those people who have difficulty receiving help, think of it as a favor to me, because I really don't want to get back to my paperwork."

"We'll help each other, then," Kerrie said. She offered a friendly smile, which Nia reciprocated. She handed Kerrie a towel and instructed her to change into it. Nia made use of the waiting time by getting the massage table ready. Having set it up last night, she only had to layer the table with padding and sheets. She finished just as Kerrie returned. When Kerrie reached the table, she went still. A sparkle lit up her eyes. I unraveled its reason by pinpointing the spot at which she was staring. Nia picked up Kerrie's pillow and handed it to her.

Kerrie hugged her pillow, but this time she was aware of doing so.

"I know this may seem silly, but I've always enjoyed having my own pillow when staying away from home. Been so bogged down, my memory of it has been gone."

"It's not silly at all. On the contrary, it's quite natural to grow attached to our belongings, because we find comfort in them. Lie down. You can use your pillow to rest your head." Kerrie took Nia up on the suggestion. She also rested her hands on top, with arms comfortably wrapped around the sides of the pillow. Meanwhile, Nia turned on some meditation music with water sounds, to play faintly in the background and set the mood.

"Considering your tiredness, aching muscles, and aforementioned memory loss, I am going to use rosemary for your massage. I refer to it as my 'one-stop shopping' essential oil because of its versatility. Its powerful properties range from mental to physical health. You said your dwindling energy was becoming bothersome, which clearly suggests the mental need for a pick up. Uplifting the mind and bringing mental clarity are among the various uses of rosemary essential oil. It is known to enhance memory and is conducive to retaining alertness."

"I certainly appreciate the clearing your head part, because of my brain fog."

"Exactly." Nia added a couple drops of rosemary essential oil to a tissue. "We will begin with aroma inhalation for the purpose of boosting all mental benefits." She held the tissue in front of Kerrie's face. "Take three deep breaths." After achieving a favorable response and subsequent stillness, Nia unfolded the towel down to Kerrie's waistline and placed a sheet on top.

"By also acting as an analgesic, it soothes aching muscles, headaches, and migraines. I've now covered all applicable remedies, so I will dispense with the talking to allow you to hear the background music during your massage, which no doubt will heighten the experience."

"Wait, I know you mentioned lavender prior to bedtime, but what did you mean, and how does it help nightmares?"

"Lavender sets a relaxing mood to bring on a peaceful sleep. Since anxiety is a known cause of nightmares, it proves to be effective. After noticing your pillow, I suggested to Alex we could add a few drops to it before bedtime. I informed Alex earlier that I had left a bottle here, since she most likely will be the one to do it."

"I love that the solution involves my pillow. Sorry to interrupt. I'm ready now."

"Thought you might, and no problem. I realize how disturbing nightmares are." Nia rubbed a blend of rosemary and coconut oil into her hands and directly applied it to Kerrie's back in a gentle, flowing motion. Nia's massage of choice was Swedish, which included a variety of techniques.

I was more than happy to sit back and witness the exchange between the two of them. I thought of it as another opportunity to study Kerrie. There were many ways to get to know someone, and I was seeking them all out. My supervisors had assigned Kerrie to me because they had believed I could connect with her. I needed to discover who she was.

In detox, knowing your patient was a necessity, because the person in your care was not acting like his or her normal self. Making a connection was crucial on the road to recovery. Connections were the catalysts for getting back to the true self he or she had become alienated from. The destination of sustainable success could only be arrived at through therapy.

My role was to get Kerrie to the starting line by building her strength and readying her for the journey. Reflecting on the day, I was encouraged that Kerrie's true nature had become more visible through verbal and physical clues. But I had to be careful not to become overzealous, which risked pushing Kerrie deeper into herself. Connecting with her was going to take as long it took, and I was okay with that. The knowledge of progress, no matter how small, would content me.

Speaking of contented, that word pretty much described Kerrie after her massage. At least physically, which indicated pain relief. Following the massage, we returned to the private balcony for an early dinner. Detox resulted in an increased appetite, which, compared to the suppressed one brought on by her addiction, was undoubtedly preferable. Kerrie could return to her previous weight safely through good nutrition.

As before, we followed our meal with a walk, but this time we spoke. Nothing more than small talk, which Kerrie initiated, but I suspected it had more to do with being polite than a desire for conversation. The suspicion came from a conversation I had had with Hazel, who told me about their first meeting and the way Kerrie's mother had recently used it as an accusation of Kerrie's rudeness. Hazel said she had never heard this opinion before, and described Kerrie's worried tone when she asked whether she had felt the same way as her mother.

The child receiving the accusation had grown into an adult who was overly conscientious about how she came across to others, especially regarding their potentially hurt feelings from miscommunication. I believed old thought patterns had resurfaced in Kerrie. I broached my belief with Kerrie via an assurance there would be no judgment of her if she'd rather not talk. I knew I was correct when she sighed with relief.

Today marked the beginning of Kerrie's improvement and, predictably, determined the schedule to be used. There was no point deviating from what worked. I presumed our pillow plan would also serve its purpose.

34

A MEETING OF MINDS

It had been a few weeks since Kerrie had first arrived, and she was looking herself again. Her body had returned to its normal weight. Aromatherapy had restored her mental and physical capacities, but she remained pensive and reticent, which was par for the course with what I had learned of Kerrie's behavior. I wanted to give Kerrie an opportunity to come around on her own, and had made an executive decision to postpone therapy.

Much of Kerrie's time was spent either looking out the window or sitting outside. In both cases, all she did was stare. Her stare appeared vacant, and her sight seemed overtaken by thoughts. Nonetheless, her mood was tranquil, and I figured it best just to leave her be.

Kim Drake, our resident psychotherapist, dropped by daily, hoping to begin behavior therapy, but I held her off because Kerrie was clearly not up to it. One of the days, Kim asked me to indulge her by letting her at least attempt a session in the room. She wanted to quiet the nagging sense that she might be able to get through to Kerrie. Kerrie tucked into her thoughts and tuned out, which settled that impression. Readiness could not be forced on anyone. Forcing it only set a person up to fail.

As usual, Kerrie had nestled into the bay window seat overlooking the rose garden, following her aromatherapy bath. This had become her morning routine before telling me it was time to get some breakfast. Seeing her now as she turned to face me, I knew the time was here.

"Hey, Alex, I'd like to eat breakfast in the garden this morning." A request for change of venue was refreshing, since she'd become such a creature of habit.

"Okay, do you want what they have prepared or something different?"

"What they've prepared is fine. Oh, and have them add a yogurt parfait." All of Kerrie's language, verbal and bodily, was listless. My colleagues were restless because Kerrie had yet to get beyond her melancholy. Believe me, I would have loved nothing more than to see the person her friends knew and loved, but melancholy could be a medium used to reach profound insight.

"I will call down and order it to go. Are you ready to head out after I place the order?"

"Sure am." Monica, Curtis's daughter, answered the phone. After I had told her Kerrie's request, she offered to bring it to us. Curtis was a proud papa, because Monica was an excellent chef in her own right. She and some friends had recently opened their own restaurant, but she periodically filled in at the rehab center to help her dad out.

"We are all set, Kerrie. Our food is going to be brought to us in the garden. Do you want to go ahead outside or watch for it in here?"

"I'm ready to get outdoors. I love how we can enter the garden area from our room." Kerrie headed down a brick walk, which circled around a classically designed gazebo that had a spindle railing on seven sides and built-in benches, all freshly painted white. White was also the color of the Victorian wicker dining set, strategically centered inside. Resting along the outer railing was a hedge of bushes interspersed with roses. The surrounding lawn was as smooth as carpet and bordered by more hedges.

I joined Kerrie at the table, sitting across from her. "Kerrie, I have not wanted to interrupt your solitude out of respect for privacy. But I'm curious if my hunch is correct—that your reason for it is to reach self-awareness."

"It is. And I appreciate your assuring me that my not talking is okay. The confidence you gave me by doing so put me at ease to allow myself to be absorbed in my musing."

"I'm glad I spoke up, then. Don't want you agonizing over acting in a way inconsistent with how you feel."

"You really get me. I would be intrigued about how that's possible, if it were not for the fact you work here. I gather you have to familiarize yourself with different personality types to be effective."

"I can't deny the insight can be a handy tool in reading people, but effectiveness can only be achieved through an accurate interpretation."

"I hear ya." We carried on with small talk during breakfast and headed back to our room after we finished. Jana opened the door for us and whispered in my ear that she had been sent to get me for a meeting. I had a sneaking suspicion I was going to be confronted regarding my resistance to therapy and told time was up on my way of handling the case.

"Kerrie, I have to go to the office for a bit, but Jana is here to hang out with you." Kerrie had settled back into the window seat, and Jana could see my confusion as to whether she had heard me or not.

"Hey Kerrie, would you like to walk down to the beach with me while Alex is in her meeting?"

"Yeah, I would."

"Great! I'm usually stuck indoors. Go on, Alex, we're good here." Both Kerrie's response and Jana's reassurance helped me feel better about leaving.

I entered the office and wasn't the least bit surprised to see Kim standing alongside Lisa. They both had intent looks on their faces, and I desperately wanted to say something that would break the ice. Nothing came to mind, so I offered a smile instead. The smile worked to some degree to lighten the serious mood, because I received one in return from each of them. Lisa motioned for us to have a seat at a glossy, oval oak table neatly tucked inside a nook.

"Alex," said Lisa, "let me start by saying Tyler has been bragging about how well you and Kerrie have been getting along. He shared that he showed up in the room the first evening, and Kerrie was concerned you were leaving. Tyler also stated Kerrie strung more words together than she had spoken earlier. And this being only her first day here. I did choose you for this case, so I can't say I'm surprised by Kerrie's quick comfort with you, but it's impressive, nonetheless. You're looking confused, Alex. What is it?"

"I am just wondering when the 'but' is going to come in."

"There is none. Why would you think that?"

"Well, you two seemed to be having a pretty serious conversation when I walked in. Combined with the fact you began with a compliment, it caused me to believe you were attempting to soften a blow."

"Oh, it's nothing like that. Kim had been filling me in on her opinion of Kerrie from information she'd received. I asked you here to update me on anything you've learned from being around her. By combining the knowledge, we can better assess what is needed to move forward. Kim, go ahead and share with Alex what you told me."

"After my experience with Kerrie, I realized I needed to do some digging for the sake of gaining the insight you instinctively have from your own experience. I hope you don't mind my bringing it up." My stay here was no secret to either of them, for two reasons. First, Lisa had been my therapist and, at the same time, had mentored Kim to assume her position before being promoted to her current role. Second, I continue to receive support through an aftercare program.

"Not at all, because it's relevant to my ability to relate to Kerrie, which is a no-brainer answer as to why I was selected. From whom did you receive your information?"

"Erin. Alex, I agree with giving Kerrie an opportunity to reach a resolve on her own. That way, she can enter therapy with a strength we can build upon. It's been several weeks, and I became curious about the plausibility of this happening. I saw in your notes that Kerrie has been in rehab previously, and called Erin with the thought that Kerrie might have shared with her information that could be useful to us. Turns out, rehab is where Kerrie began writing, which became her purpose."

"I knew it!" I said, increasing my volume. "Sorry, I presumed as much. I also believe writing gave Kerrie an outlet for reinventing herself."

"You are so right, Alex. Erin mentioned Kerrie said she reinvented herself from the purpose she found through writing."

"I wasn't aware she started in rehab, but then again, I didn't much wonder about it. Getting back to your curiosity about Kerrie's potential for resolve, what did Erin reveal?"

"Right," said Kim, "she spoke of witnessing Kerrie at a couple of low points. In each case, Kerrie reverted, but through conversation was able to return to herself because of a reminder of who she's become." An earlier discussion between Erin and me popped into my head.

"Are you still with us, Alex?" asked Lisa. "You appear to be off somewhere else."

"I was just thinking about an earlier exchange with Erin. Getting back to the point, you're saying Kerrie has reverted and will remain stuck in this state without help. But you saw her drawn deep into her thoughts, and I even referred to it as solitude when questioning her earlier."

"Wait," interrupted Kim, "you and Kerrie discussed it? Tell me also about your talk with Erin, because something I said obviously sparked the memory."

"Wouldn't call it a discussion, really. She merely confirmed my hunch that the solitude was a way to self-awareness. I based the choice to give Kerrie her space on my hunch. Regarding Erin, after relaying my story to her and Kirk because of the glaring similarities, she asked if I would share it with Kerrie."

"Bingo!" Lisa yelled, abruptly halting me from speaking further.

"What, you think I should?"

"Yes, but continue, because my gut tells me you will say something to prompt Kim's opinion on the matter."

"That's about it, except for addressing what sparked my recollection. Kim, because of my response to Erin, your point about a reminder returning Kerrie to herself jogged my memory. In my conversation with Erin, I included some acquired insight along with my anecdote, and insisted it was nothing Kerrie didn't already know. She would just need to be reminded of it, and that reminder would come in therapy. With all of Kerrie's inwardness, she was nowhere near ready for therapy. I hoped her own awareness could get her there, because I feared interfering might just drive her in deeper."

"That's a legitimate concern, Alex," Kim said. "And one I had shared up until talking with Erin. I believe this recent trauma has Kerrie floundering again in a cloudy sea of childhood emotions of hurt and despair, which are preventing her from thinking her way clear of them. I now fear not interfering will bring about our concern."

All that Kim said made perfect sense and brought to the forefront knowledge from different sources, including my own observations. Well aware that my time to update Lisa and Kim was drawing near, I tried my best to piece together all the information so I could present it with a semblance of coherence. Absorbed in my task, I barely heard Lisa call my name and, as expected, request my update.

"I want to respond regarding the issue of childhood emotions, for their cause is the key to fixing the faulty thinking that Kerrie still carries with her today. The burden of misperception that weighs on Kerrie impressed itself at an early age. As a result, she's become an adult who is overly concerned that negative connotation will be attached to her intention."

"You're talking about the accusation that she was rude, based on her silence and despite a smile, which was rehashed in the latest confrontation between Kerrie and her mom," said Kim.

"Correct. I see you've read my notes."

"No. I mean, yes, regarding your notes on Helen's side of the story. But I was speaking more about Erin's synopsis of Kerrie's recent recollection of the initial scene, which was triggered by a similar incident she witnessed."

"Is this one of the low points Erin referred to?" I asked, with keen interest. I was chomping at the bit, curious about the details, but, in the interest of time, thought better of asking.

"Yes. Erin described the hurt Kerrie had felt and relived through her flashback. It's the same hurt I alluded to earlier. She also mentioned that she spoke to you of the similarities between you and Kerrie without delving into specifics. This part was reported in the file, along with your intention to follow up with her. No additional annotations were made, but you've been a little preoccupied lately. I concluded following up had been less important. On the other hand, with Kerrie not being ready for me, I was available to follow up with Erin. The direct and indirect approaches we're taking toward understanding are proving to be effective in highlighting common descriptions of Kerrie gathered from separate experiences with her. Having said that, I want to touch upon what you said earlier. Alex, do you have anything to add before I do?"

"You are right, Kim, that my preoccupation reduced the importance of my desire to follow up. I'm glad you did, though, because you unknowingly uncovered my impetus for wanting to do so."

"What impetus? You're going to leave it there? You really think I'd be able to continue after your dropping a statement like that?"

"I was thinking more along the lines of being brief so you could get back to where you left off." Kim and Lynn had their eyes glued to me, strongly implying my explanation had not been satisfactory enough to move on. "Erin told me about getting Kerrie to open up after an episode of cathartic crying. Naturally, I was motivated to get to the root of what had caused Kerrie to be so upset. But it had to wait, because I'd already taken up a lot of time, and needed to get back and check on her. Most likely, the flashback is connected to the root, and I would love to hear the whole account. But again, I find myself anxious to get back to Kerrie. Or, better yet, I can read your documentation."

"Yes, you can. You're probably right. All the dots are connecting nicely and becoming a visual we can work with. Stands to reason the flashback is the root you were hoping to pull out. To your point from earlier, the incident laid the groundwork from which faulty thinking festered. Words and phrasing can carry a dual meaning. Even when the delivery expresses a positive intention, if the recipient's psyche has been damaged by social, cultural, or personal experience, he or she may infer a negative connotation. A common example is that kidding can often come across as an insult.

"Kerrie, having a sensitivity to this, can easily find herself reeling with analytical thoughts about what she is about to say or has just finished saying. The result is she either carefully chooses her words or proactively puts an unquestionably positive spin on those already spoken, the burden of which is not her responsibility to bear. But, in truth, the responsibility of interpretation lies solely with the one who breathes life into negative connotations, and the job of changing a mind that naturally inclines toward them rests here, as well. I don't imagine Kerrie would ever again believe not speaking was an option. Alex, you would be a better judge of that."

"Well, I certainly have experience with my own self-inflicted mental drama. Your accurate portrayal is a sad commentary on how a person can try to control one aspect of life by predicting reactions to avoid confrontation. So, Kim, about the not speaking option, the answer is no. The consequence of this choice was branded on Kerrie's brain, producing a determination never to relive it and a wish to be well thought of. We can't really count her early days here—though awake, she was still out of it. After the haze lifted, however, she engaged me in small talk during one of our walks, which had previously been silent excursions. I chalked Kerrie's chattiness up to the reemergence of old thought patterns, which prompted her to choose etiquette over a desire for silence. Kerrie's wish to be likable has her attempting to steer clear of any actions that might give off a bad impression."

"Hmm," Lisa said, "who does that sound like?" I chuckled, knowing what Lisa was getting at. Through Kerrie, I saw glimpses of my own ritualistic behaviors, which before therapy had not seemed to me abnormal. I had considered it common decency to consider the feelings of others by conceptualizing how I might come across negatively and, accordingly, acting in such a way that would prevent and neutralize repercussions. If I failed to do so, I believed any unease I felt was deserved.

"Well, it's been a real eye-opener, for sure, to view this case from your standpoint and see what I must have been like. Another motive of yours, I presume." A triumphant smirk spread across Lisa's face.

"I'd like to think of it as a method for recovery maintenance. Anyhow, I take it you've substantiated your assertion that Kerrie's chattiness had more to do with politeness than a desire for conversation."

"Yes, I gave Kerrie my assurance there'd be no judgment of her if she'd rather not talk. I received verification in the form of a sigh of relief. Furthermore, just this morning, Kerrie voiced appreciation for my assuring her about not talking, which put her at ease and allowed her to become absorbed in her musing." Kim had been listening with earnest and eager attention, as if waiting to hear the very thing that would prompt her to pounce with a response. Seeing as her eyes had just widened, I knew my last remark had struck a chord.

"Kerrie actually used the term 'musing'?"

"Yes. I don't know if this is important, but it was right after confirming my self-awareness theory."

"I believe it is, because here's what I'm thinking. Musing can suggest either introspection or daydreaming. There is a mental element to daydreaming that takes us away from stress. This method to retreat from reality is sometimes done knowingly, but other times the mind wanders away on its own."

"Wow! The mind is amazing. I get where you're going with this. Kerrie's attempts at self-awareness are being interrupted or blocked by her mind's need for escape, corroborating your theory about her floundering, and bringing us right back to dissociation. And I'd been cheerleading for her success. The gratification derived would have been a boost to her next level of recovery."

"Exactly! And I'd be cheerleading right alongside you if I thought it possible for her to succeed on her own. The floundering, which I attributed to hurt and despair, is most likely the result of those same feelings setting off a warning alarm in Kerrie's mind, which promptly shuts down. Unlike the dissociation we witnessed at her admittance, this time it's involuntary. The good news is that she's still striving for any morsel of self-awareness."

"Yeah, especially after what she's been through. And the most inconceivable aspect of it all is that Kerrie believed her mother had died, leaving shattered glass in her wake. And she came through all that, save for the occasional shards of anguish that jabbed at her, only to find out that she's still alive." As I spoke, my mind raced back to my own figurative death experience with my mother.

That she refused to take responsibility for or even acknowledge her actions and the ways they had hurt me killed our relationship. The mere suggestion had her feigning hysteria with an Academy Award-worthy performance. Her tearfully expressed hurt swiftly turned into indignation. Can't say I'd expected anything different, really, but I'd still hoped she could be somewhat reasonable. "What's good for the goose is good for the gander," I'd thought, since she'd never once hesitated to call me on the carpet and spew the countless ways in which I had wronged her.

It was this behavior that had stuck in my craw and had me break the silence of how I'd been wronged. At college, my best friend, Maxine, exposed my mother and freed me to know that she had wronged me. My intention had not been to rehash the past, but to have a calm and open dialogue. I had planned to relinquish sole proprietorship of blame and find mutual, common ground in our shared responsibility. Obviously, this had not been the case, and at this point I felt certain I had just added to her list.

My forthrightness could also have been credited, in part, to my need to finally untie the knot my life had been tied in. The knot had made me hold back my true feelings because of how I felt certain they would be received. I was neither sure her reproach that I was too sensitive wasn't entirely accurate nor certain her punishments—of blame, criticism, and emotional blackmail—were outside the realm of normal parenting. Without a reference point, I had remained tied up in their plausibility. The frustration that built up in me ultimately released itself on something that would be, in the grand scheme of things, unimportant.

But at least this time I had been attempting to address the real issues of my life, a situation that ended with my mother screaming her grocery list of my mistakes in chronological order. And, yes, as suspected, this confrontation finished off the list. I had returned to college feeling even lower, catapulting me deep into a world of addiction, which had brought me here. And here was where I needed to return, to refocus on Kerrie and break the pause in conversation, just as I had broken my silence so many years before.

Looking at Lisa and Kim, I saw them slowly emerge from the journey their own thoughts had taken them on. "So, where do we go from here?" I said, hoping to hasten their return.

"Well!" Lisa and Kim exclaimed simultaneously, lifting the apparent trance they had been under. They stalled. After a brief delay, Kim spoke first. "Sorry, Alex. To determine where we go from here, I had to first consider all possible solutions. As stated earlier, Kerrie needs help to get unstuck, and I still contend your sharing your story is the best answer."

"I agree," said Lisa. "Nothing I've heard has weakened that opinion, only strengthened it. How about you, Alex? Anything troubling you?"

"No, I'm good, now that my nerves about this meeting have settled down."

"Glad to hear it. If there is nothing further to discuss, we are done here." At that, knowing the task at hand and feeling eager to start, I pushed back my chair and headed for the door. I was ready to resume my work.

35

SHEDDING SOME LIGHT

Standing on the edge of the cliff, I noted where Kerrie and Jana had positioned themselves, before heading down to join them. They were both sitting on low beach chairs placed in the ocean. The sight of Kerrie reclining with legs stretched out, soaking up the sun as water streamed over her feet, gave her the appearance of not having a care in the world. It made me pause with the realization I had raced out here and had no clue how to proceed. I began rehearsing lines in my head, to no avail. Just as well, because sometimes letting conversations happen naturally was best.

I proceeded down the stone pathway and, upon reaching the sand, removed my shoes to make the remaining distance easier to walk. And because I liked the feel of sand beneath my feet. I moved in a diagonal direction to reach them. Jana must have caught movement in her peripheral vision, because she turned toward me.

"Alex!" Jana yelled, alerting Kerrie of my presence. Kerrie turned to me with a smile, and then leaped off her chair and gave me a tight hug.

"I'm so glad you're back, Alex," Kerrie finally said, in a whisper. "You are back, right? I realize I've not been exactly responsive, and recognize you've been easygoing with me. I hope you didn't get in any trouble because of it."

"All is good. And yes, I'm back," I answered, with a reassuring tone meant to defuse Kerrie's fearful one.

"It's just that you've been gone for a while."

"Well, I have yet to experience a brief meeting. Don't believe such a thing truly exists. In fact, the word 'meeting' should be synonymous with 'prolonged length of time' and make the combination an oxymoron." Kerrie listened with thoughtful consideration, until a slight nod revealed she related to what I was saying.

"Don't let Kerrie fool you, Alex," Jana said. "From the instant you walked out the door, she began fretting, asking me if there was a problem. A question, no doubt, whose conclusion she'd already jumped to, and I could tell guilt had already taken its place. Nonetheless, I felt the need to attempt to calm her, albeit futilely, by stating everything was fine. I even attempted to joke, like you did, about brief meetings, so that the passing of time wouldn't further fuel her already worked-up state." I realized Kerrie's nod had related to my reiteration of Jana's point.

"You both looked, to me, as tranquil as the waters."

"Yeah, well, I'd like to take credit, but the ocean has that effect. But then again, I did suggest coming down here, so I'll take the credit after all."

"You did help me, Jana," Kerrie piped up. "Sorry it didn't show, but the lighthearted personality you and Alex have does make me feel better. It connects me to how I used to be, which gives me comfort. I want to get back to being that way, and feel like I'm trying, but can't seem to get there." I was elated with

Kerrie's frankness. So much so that my mind wandered off with the good fortune of this much-needed opening.

"Anyways, did everything really go okay, Alex?"

"Alex!" shouted Jana.

"What?"

"Kerrie asked you a question. And I'm also interested in the answer. Did everything—"

"Yes," I interrupted. Jana's question had dawned on me before she had finished repeating it. I don't know how the brain stores information when you're not even paying attention. At least not that you're aware of. "Let's get back to the room, and I'll fill you in." Jana and Kerrie folded their chairs and returned them to the beach storage cabin.

Walking back, I imagined how our conversation might go. I didn't wonder so much about what I would say, because I'd already decided to have the talk play out naturally, but rather about how the heart-to-heart would go. The walk's silence was a strong indicator that we were all accompanied by similar thoughts. My earlier concern that Kerrie would retreat further into herself had been eased when she opened the door for me to share my experience. Her willingness boded well for a positive outcome.

Upon arriving back in the room, Jana's pager went off, and she excused herself. Kerrie returned to the comforts of the window seat, and I joined her, noticing her scrutiny on me. Given her avidity for what I was about to say, I dove right in.

"Okay, Kerrie, I think the best place to start would be with the comment you made about your attempts to get back to being lighthearted but finding yourself unable to get there. It corroborates Kim's hypothesis of you being stuck. Do you remember speaking of being absorbed in your musing?" Kerrie's eyes glazed over, revealing her answer. "It was in connection with my putting you at ease."

"Oh! About not talking, right?"

"Yes. Well, the mere mention of the word 'musing' lit Kim up like a contestant on a game show."

"Haha! Great analogy, Alex. Just visualized a comedic skit."

"That's funny! Can see it myself. Anyhoo, Kim informed me that musing can suggest introspection or daydreaming. She went on to elaborate that there is a mental element to daydreaming that takes us away from stress. It's a method of retreating from reality, either activated knowingly or resulting from the mind wandering away on its own."

"Whoa! Do you believe that's happening to me?"

"I suggested to Kim, for the purposes of clarifying my understanding, that your attempts at self-awareness are being interrupted or blocked by the mind's need for escape, leaving you floundering. Kim theorized that the floundering is linked to your emotions setting off, as she put it, a warning alarm in your mind, after which it promptly shuts down." I could see relief blanket Kerrie as she digested the information.

"That certainly explains the quicksand feeling. I've been striving for a destination my mind obstructed me from reaching. Does that about sum it up?"

"Just about. Further understanding will come with Kim."

"And I expect you're to encourage me to begin therapy. I'm comforted there is a reason for my inability to cope, but don't think I can." I didn't need to ask about the problem. The calm Kerrie initially spoke with had veered off into detectable discomfort. Kerrie's eyes had grown heavy under the weight of knowing the work therapy would ask of her. She began massaging her temples in response to the fear-induced pressure pounding in her head. It was the fear of being unable to meet the session's expectations. And her body had hunched over with the concern that unshakable low spirits would deplete the resources needed to get better.

"You can relax, Kerrie. Ultimately, therapy is the plan, but there is no urgency to begin. So stop worrying about the sessions. And you will get better." Kerrie glanced up at me in surprise. She appeared to be settling down, but was now rubbing her forehead. A familiar sight that caused me to move confidently to get her some aspirin.

"It's almost as if I'm thinking out loud with you. You must have had several clients already to be able to read thoughts so well."

"Nope. Four?"

"Only four clients?" Apparently, my timing caused the question mark in my tone to go unnoticed, especially since I had gotten up without any clarification as to what I was doing.

"No. No, that was a question to confirm the number of aspirin. You've been rubbing your head, and I remember you mentioned four does the trick."

"Yes, you remembered correctly. Didn't even realize I was doing that. Guess over the years it's become my reflexive, go-to response to lessen the headache." I pulled down my duffle bag from the top of the closet and got the aspirin. On the way back, I grabbed a bottle of water from the fridge. I wanted to wait to begin until Kerrie had digested the aspirin and could give me her full attention. While I was waiting, I threw in a deep breath for good measure.

"Automatic responses are yet another example of how the mind controls us without our awareness. And, to be perfectly honest with you, I have assisted with many clients, but you're the first client I've been assigned to. Deliberately assigned, I should say. You see, contrary to your belief, my ability to read you does not come from knowledge gained from different personality types, but rather..." I paused for emphasis, taking another deep breath, "from sitting in your place." I had piqued Kerrie's interest. Her eyes concentrated on mine in fervent anticipation.

"Lisa chose me because she was my therapist during my stay here, making her fully aware of the similarities between us. Simply put, my relationship with my mother is also a painful one. She fiercely needed to be in control, and could only be nurtured by her ability to do so. She deemed this ability a measure of love and my desire to please her an expression of that love. I was asked in therapy if I perceived the love I received in return to be a reward for obeying."

"That's a germane question. What was your answer?" Kerrie asked. I doubted she was purely focused on my response, because the nature of the subject matter was bound to make her question how she would answer.

"It was, but sadly I did not have an answer. I tried to think back to my perspective as a child, but this offered no help. Remembered just doing what I was told. Not much thought process goes into that. Lisa described this as a typical childhood response due to subliminal conditioning processes. She rephrased the question, specifying the age at which repetitive negativity began to play on my psyche. I'll stop here to say I can't claim to know all the negativity you experienced, but I can assert that the emotions it evoked are the same."

"You may be right, but currently I'm blown away by your disclosure. With your confident disposition, I would never have guessed."

"Ha! Erin said as much, which is not surprising given best friends' usage of similar phrasing. Now, you're probably wondering why I didn't think to share with you sooner." Kerrie nodded in the affirmative.

"I believed giving you the space necessary to reach a level of self-awareness was vital to moving toward therapy. The space where answers will be found and the prior awareness you've been having difficulty accessing will be activated." Kerrie's silence spoke to the fact she had jumped onto my train of thought and did not want to get off until I came to a complete stop. "Erin needed to understand what you were going through, and I used my experience to help her. At the same time, I wanted to reassure both her and Kirk about your outcome by telling my story."

"I totally get your reasoning, but can't help wondering if it's hard to talk about."

"Erin raised that question, too. No, because bringing up my situation to enlighten others keeps me from reliving the emotions."

"In that case, I'm curious to know if Lisa's rephrasing helped?"

"It did. By referencing the negativity, memories came to life, dredging up my mindset. In my mind's eye, I don't recall thinking about love received, which is why I was thrown by the initial question. It had more to do with the treatment I received from my mother, which clearly indicated whether my actions were good or bad." Kerrie raised an eyebrow, a "tell" that I had touched upon something. By keeping her engaged with my experience, I was providing a painless way for Kerrie to get back to herself.

"The times I fell short of meeting expectations left me defenseless against venomous daggers stabbing me with condemnation. Could not see beyond the bottom line to know my mother was acting unreasonably. I had upset her, which, to me, made her reaction justifiable. The shame from disappointing would come and go, but the cuts of criticism continued to sting. A war raged within me about the validity of my hurt, leading me to feel inadequate for not being able to get over it. Like I said, I believed her behavior to be justified. Therefore, it must have been me. At this point, I'd like to continue by addressing your other curiosities."

"Thanks, Alex. I would just like to know how deep our similarities go. So, what brought you here?"

"Ah! Then I suppose you'd also like to know if my mom raised me alone, but you're too polite to ask. When I was five, my dad died in a car accident driving home from work."

"I'm so sorry! You're right, I was curious, but didn't ask because I was afraid it might be something bad."

"I figured as much. Anyway, like you, stimulants. Speed, mostly, but later moved on to coke. The timing of which I won't get into now, because it will come up eventually. At any rate, knowing a little of my background, I'm sure you probably have questions."

"Yeah. Did you use because of responsibility and guilt, or did you realize the madness?"

"Both, actually. When I started in college, my ability to focus was severely impacted by the pressures of responsibility, which fired me up with guilt. My continued use related to the madness, which I could not fully realize until I began socializing a bit with fellow students. Prior to that, I pretty much remained isolated."

"How did your mother feel about you going away to college?"

"Fine. It gave her bragging rights, but not because of her pride in me. My getting into Stanford reflected well upon her, shining the spotlight on herself."

"I see, but I'm sure she had a hard time with you moving out. Being so reliant on you and all."

"We lived close enough for me to commute, which is primarily why I applied there. Despite what you may think, my having a social life did not bother her. Only became an issue if it took priority over being there for her. And having a job helped me cover my own expenses, which was good for us both."

"You intimated the environment exposed the craziness of your life, giving you a dose of a reality check."

"Definitely. Had some friends who expressed wanting to hang out with me more. The freedom they had to lead separate lives from their parents opened my eyes to the fact my identity was of my mother's making, not my own. A thread of reason was on the edge of unraveling. Collectively, they all smiled politely when I explained why I could not, but my best friend, Maxine, pulled me aside and minced no words when telling me how fucked up my explanation was. That my mother was ludicrous and I was living in insanity because of her. Ding, ding, ding! Max introduced me to reality."

"Betting your explanation revealed more to Max than what you said."

"Yeah, she informed me I was living in a bubble in my belief that complying with my mother's wishes was the right thing to do and that her expectations were reasonable."

"Wow! Was Maxine a psychology major, or did she live through the same issues? And did this clear up the doubt you struggled with over your inability to get over your hurt? Sorry to bombard you with so many questions." Evidently, Kerrie was now energized, and I'd like to think it had something to do with the edginess of her situation being lifted.

"You're fine. The crash course Max gave me on manipulation tactics cleared up my doubt, helping me to see my hurt as valid. So much so that I calmly confronted my mother in the hopes of clearing the air and possibly paving a way to having a true relationship. I was naïve in thinking my objective could be remotely possible. Hope springs eternal."

"Didn't go well, I take it."

"Not so much. My attempts to reason with her so she could see my side of things were canceled out by her inability to acknowledge the existence of a problem. Guess it was hard to recognize a problem when the relationship was going along as she felt it should. She took my seeing it differently as a direct attack and, accordingly, played the victim, moving from a tearful, quivering voice to shouting in record time. An ugly scene turned into an even uglier scene.

"Needless to say, my friends got their wish. They were all renting a house, and I moved in. What happened next will answer your question about Max. I took partying beyond a social level and, one day, Max came home to find me crashed out on the floor beside our coffee table. The supplies on the table made what I'd been up to obvious. Unable to wake me, she panicked and called her sister, Lisa. Now you're up to speed, no pun intended. Let's eat, I'm starving."

"I here ya, and could also eat." We both headed for the door. "And I got your point. Max undoubtedly gained insight from Lisa, and Lisa is how you came to be here." The fact that Kerrie was keen on understanding my life was a step in the right direction. "I can appreciate what you've told me, Alex, but I'm still not ready for therapy." Just saying the word "therapy" caused Kerrie to tense up.

"Didn't expect you would be. That's okay, because I have an idea. You still have your book to finish, right? Well, we offer creative writing among other healing services designed to get you back on track. What better way to reconnect you to your life than jumping into the job that made it all possible?" Kerrie's bright-eyed reaction proved she liked the idea. "No pressure, it's just a thought."

"You're right, Alex. I do need to finish my book, and writing did help me before. Stands to reason it would have the same effect. Yeah. I want to do that." While we ate, we went over the plans to get her started, and afterward I arranged to get her laptop.

36

BREAKTHROUGH

I was back to myself. Many of the days here had been a blur. I knew I had started off with detox. For how long, I didn't know. Length of time escaped me. Erin delivered what Maria had packed for the remainder of my stay. That was when she dropped off my laptop. I was glad I didn't have many bills and that they were set up online. Erin asked if there was anything she could do for me. Paying Maria and Antonio was the only thing I could come up with, and was relieved to hear she'd already taken care of that.

I had several therapy sessions that helped. Kim, my therapist, informed me that she had started off by attempting a session in my room, but she had not been able to reach me. I had no recollection of this.

Kim went on to say that my rate of progress had made up for lost time. I had even finished my book, which had gotten me back in my element and settled my nerves, allowing for a smooth transition to therapy and accelerating my recovery. With the progress I'd made, Kim told me she could very easily put in a recommendation for my release soon. That was music to my ears. I was anxious to go home and get back to my life, so I hoped that by getting to Kim early and participating even more, I might expedite a discharge date.

Kim's door was open. Before I could knock, she looked up from her desk and saw me.

"Hey, Kerrie. You're early, but we can go ahead and get started, if you like."

"I'm ready if you are." Walked over and plopped down on the sofa.

"Okay then." Kim got up to sit in the chair across from me. "Let's start by reviewing. You previously shared that your mother accused you of stealing your dad and grandfather from her. Your last statement yesterday was that while you understood she was being irrational, her words still hurt. We were out of time and had to end there. This is where I want to start. How is that hurt now?"

"Much less. It was all consuming before, but my mind is no longer clouded."

"Good. I have noticed that. Do you understand why your mom lashed out?"

"Not specifically, still don't totally understand the underlying cause of her problems, but I will tell you that the behavior exhibited was explained to me years ago. I was told about lashing out in order to draw people in, but ultimately pushing them away."

"Yes. A self-fulfilling prophecy. Sounds to me like your mother has strong issues related to abandonment. Her fear is so severe that she creates the situation, which brings it about. The fear becoming a reality justifies the fear. There is an inability to recognize or take blame for the chaos created by her unrealistic expectations. Primarily because your mother does not view the expectations as unrealistic, a result of her sense of entitlement. Therefore, she believes her reaction to their not being met is justifiable. A victim mentality resurfaces, another tactic to draw people in, as you put it."

"Wow! That makes sense. Is it possible that the need for control represents a test of loyalty or proof of love? If so, can someone feel abandoned after losing that ability to control?"

"Very good, Kerrie. I can see the benefit of Alex's talk with you. Someone like your mother perceives the loss of control over another person as a lack of attention from that person. This perceived inattentiveness also translates to abandonment. These people believe the world revolves around them, and project a false persona meant to conceal the truth that they feel unloved and unlovable. They conceal this truth not only from others but also from themselves, avoiding the pain that results from a fragile self-image.

"To this end, control manifests with many manipulative faces. It satiates a ceaseless need to be constantly catered to, with helpings of attention that no one could sustain without sacrificing his or her own life. On the flip side, choosing a life that does not involve constantly placating someone else—well, let's just say it only takes one faulty wheel to upset the apple cart. The faulty wheel, in this case, represents any decision that might indicate another primary focus."

"Alex shared something along those lines. I'm paraphrasing, but it had to do with issues arising from changing priorities. At any rate, I imagine loneliness can be experienced in a crowded room, if attention is not received. I feel lost because of all the negativity from the chaos created. The inability to make a difference or change the situation, and being attacked with brutal criticism as a result of that failure, swallows me whole. Reality escapes me and is replaced with despair. I think that's it."

"What is it, Kerrie? Also, you're right about the crowded room analogy."

"Despair. I experience it to such an extreme degree that I become lost and spiral out of control."

"Keep going. Think that point through."

"I guess being lost leads me to a quiet place for comfort. I can only reach that place when trying to find a cure for my uneasiness. The emotional pain suffered triggers my addiction."

"Exactly! Understanding your addiction is a big part of recovery. The other part is identifying the tools that help you handle stress and triggers. I believe you discovered those tools years ago. Do you remember them? From what you stated earlier, I gather helping people is very important to you."

"I discovered reading helps me. Found it to be a source of comfort. This led to my desire to write, in hopes of helping others. I then had a purpose, which gave me an identity related to me. Went from being a daughter to a granddaughter. Apart from that, did not know who I was. Writing helped me know myself."

"Did you always feel that way?"

"No. Was fine before we moved."

"Why do you think that is?"

"Our neighbors, friends, and their parents voiced their enthusiasm when calling out my name."

"What did the enthusiasm signify to you?"

"It signified a closeness they felt for me. So, I guess my identity came from that closeness. Lost that when we moved, and writing gave it back to me."

"Okay, Kerrie."

"Okay, meaning time's up?"

"Time is up, but I meant I feel you're ready to go home."

"When?"

"Now. Already made the arrangements. I was confident today you'd reach the breakthrough you needed to be released. I've already notified Erin, and she is packing your things as we speak. Remember to stay true to yourself, and you'll be fine. Call me if you need to." Kim handed me her card. "And one last thing. I didn't instruct you on boundaries, because I don't imagine you plan on contacting your mom, considering how things ended. I don't recommend it, either, based on the interaction not being safe. I only bring it up in the event your mother contacts you, which will make a boundary discussion applicable."

"Thank you, Kim. I assure you, if that happens, you will definitely be hearing from me." Leaped up, took the card, and gave her a hug. Before leaving, I looked up to the clock on the wall and made note of the time, which clued me in on where I could find Alex.

She had been reassigned to floating detail after my full time care was reduced to check-up status. At this time every day, Alex took her break. She had made it a custom to locate herself in the parlor, curled up in her favorite chair, reading the latest novel recommended to her. Angled away from me, she was so engrossed in her book that it was convenient for me to sneak behind her and wrap my arms around her for a tight hug. Alex turned and jumped up with delight upon seeing me, and then motioned for me to have a seat.

"Kerrie, is it true you're to be discharged?"

"Yes, Kim just gave me the news, and I came straight here to find you."

"So, you're saying I'm predictable," Alex stated, with an amused smirk. "Well, I'm glad I am, because I'd hoped you'd come see me before you left. My whereabouts not being a mystery saved you time finding me, so your departure won't be too delayed. I am not going to say goodbye, though, since I plan on seeing you again with each follow-up visit." She then added, with her smile turning upside down, "Still, I will miss you terribly."

"Alex, that will not do. We need to get together more than that. I want you to come over and hang out with Erin and me." My invitation lit up her face, and I hoped this meant an acceptance would follow.

"Are you serious? I would love that."

"Of course. Erin told me, during a visit, about how instantly fond of you she became, and mentioned having your card. And this was after I told her about the closeness I felt toward you. We then simultaneously blurted out we needed to invite you over. We have a plan. I'll call you and set up a date. Us birds of a feather must flock together."

"That we are, and that we must. Will do," Alex agreed, and stood up with extended arms. "One last hug before you meet Erin. And tell her hello from me."

"Okay," I said, fulfilling Alex's request, then hurrying back to my room. Erin had finished packing and was sitting on the edge of my bed. "Erin!"

"Hey, Kerrie! You look great!" We gave each other a hug.

"I feel great! And Alex told me to pass a hello onto you."

"Ah! How sweet. We must have her hang out with us."

"Yeah, I told Alex we wanted her to, and she shared our enthusiasm." Erin immediately smiled. "Guess I scared Kirk away, ha?"

"Hey, babe. Why would you think that?" I was excited to hear his voice, but reserved in showing it, and slowly turned around.

"Did not know you were behind me. Anyway, because they only told me Erin was here."

"Can't get rid of me that easy. I was just signing you out." I now felt secure enough to show my excitement, and gave Kirk a smile.

"Now that's the smile I like to see. Nice to see my girl back. Let's get you home." I liked the sound of that. Erin picked up her phone.

"We are ready. Pull up front." We exited the building. Davide quickly got out of the car and raced around to open the door for Erin. He then glanced over at me.

"Glad to have you back, Kerrie. Erin missed you."

"I am looking forward to getting home, and missed my neighbor big time. Need to return to our evening drinks." Davide got back in the driver's seat and popped the trunk. Kirk opened my door, before placing my bags in the trunk. I had kept my pillow, which still carried the aroma of lavender.

"I would love that," responded Erin. "Is that allowed?" Davide started up the car. Soon, I would be home. Finally!

"Yes. Alcohol is not my drug of choice. I initially took the stimulants to be able to help my mother during the day and gain the energy I needed to work on my book through the night. The chronic uptight feeling I was having disappeared. I felt great, and my desire to sustain that feeling kept me using. Did not want to admit that to myself."

"I imagine the environment didn't help. Probably a trigger for you."

"It was. Negativity is toxic. I fell back into a role of wanting to please, like when I was a child. Lost myself in this role, and was lured in by the times I did please. Knew this time I would need to work harder at dealing with my hurt feelings. Stimulants became my cure-all."

"Nice to see you back to yourself!"

"Thanks, Erin. Just needed to find my way back to who I've become. I understand my triggers and must remember to stay true to myself. Remaining focused on my purpose will help me handle the triggers. I want to help people, and believe writing is the means to do that. I have found comfort in reading and feel writing allows me to pass it on. Being here, with all of you, is important to me. Don't ever want to lose sight of that again. You are my family."

"I love you, Kerrie, and now we are home," said Erin. We pulled into Erin's driveway. I opened the door and got out.

Enjoyed the walk to my porch, and saw a welcome home banner stretched high across the columns. "See you later, Kerrie," yelled Erin.

"Okay, Erin." Kirk was getting my bags, which included my luggage and laptop. I couldn't wait for him, because I was eager to get inside.

I entered the foyer, placing my pillow on the side table. Maria and Antonio met me at the door with a warm embrace. "Welcome home, Kerrie," said Maria.

"We've missed you, Miss Kerrie," added Antonio.

"Missed the both of you, too! So nice to finally be home. I've been away too long." Felt a tug on my pants and looked down. Nicky was looking up at me with her big brown eyes, and was holding a card up to me.

"Hi, Kewee. I made dis for you."

"Well hello, Nicky. Thank you for my card. I love it. You draw very good."

"I know." Nicky beamed proudly, and I took her by the hand.

"I think this should go on the refrigerator. Want to help me?"

"A ha." Nicky pulled me to the kitchen and I lifted her up. Maria and Antonio entered soon after, holding hands. Their marriage was a love story seen through the affection they showed for each other, and the brightness gleaned from watching their daughter manifested an extension of that love.

"Pick out a magnet."

"I like dis wun." I handed her the card, and she stuck the magnet to it. Then she pointed to her picture. "Dats you, Kewee. I dwew you and me.

"Looks just like us, Nicky."

"I know." Again, Nicky beamed with pride.

"I made you dinner. Left it in the refrigerator for you to heat up when you're ready," said Maria. I put Nicky down.

"Come on, Nicky," said Antonio.

"K, Dadee. Bye, Kewee."

"Bye, Nicky. Come back soon." Antonio lifted Nicky.

"Bye, Miss Kerrie."

"Bye, Antonio."

"Bye, Kerrie. Eat."

"I will, and thanks, Maria. The place looks great. See you both tomorrow." After they left, I stood at the sliding door in the family room. Was admiring my yard when Kirk came up behind me.

"You okay, babe?"

"Yes. I'm enjoying being home. Seems like I've been gone forever." An idea entered my head. "Go on out, Kirk, and I will join you in a minute." Kirk slid the door open and exited. I went to the bedroom, changed into the skimpy red bathing suit Kirk had bought for me, and returned. Kirk was sitting at the wet bar and had fixed himself a drink. I slid the door open, which got Kirk's attention.

"Do you like your purchase, Kirk?"

"I do like my purchase, but love it on you." Kirk had a great smile, and he was wearing one now.

"Are you okay? You were awfully quiet while we were driving."

"I'm fine now that you're back, but I do have something to say. You probably have an idea what it is."

"I scared the hell out of you."

"That's it. Didn't help when they told me you were out of it."

"I don't remember. It's all a fog. I know it's not in my nature to stay down. I get tired of feeling bad, eventually, and want to feel better. Guess it just took me longer to come around this time. I was totally consumed with my hurt, and imagine that tuned everything else out. My mind was definitely clouded.

"Sorry I scared you, but I'm better now. I can't handle being exposed to negative environments or people for any amount of time. It's too toxic for me, and there lies the triggers. As long as I am in close proximity to all that keeps me connected to myself, I will be fine." I moved closer to Kirk. He wrapped his arms around my waist and pulled me in closer. I placed my hands on his shoulders.

"Am I included on that list?"

"Absolutely!"

"Relieved to hear that, babe." Kirk finished his drink and put the glass down. "You look great! Like I said before, nice to see my girl back."

Kirk stood up and kissed my forehead. "I would love to stay, but have some loose ends to tie up. Your book is sure to be another hit, by the way. Thanks for emailing me a copy."

"I was hoping you would like it. Will I see you later?"

"I do, and will be back tomorrow. Erin will be over later, and it might be nice to enjoy the place to yourself on your first day back."

"No offense, but you're probably right."

"None taken, babe. You will see me tomorrow."

"Okay. Bye, Kirk." Kirk left, and I headed to the pool. Took a dip and knew Kirk was right. It was nice having the place to myself. Was sitting in my grotto when I noticed Erin on her way over. Swam to the steps and got out to join her. "Hey, Erin."

"Hey back, Kerrie. Gosh, I missed you." Grabbed a towel from the supply cabinet and dried off. Put my arm around Erin as we approached the bar and took my usual position behind it to serve us drinks. "Is Kirk gone?"

"Yes. Told me he would see me tomorrow. So, how are you and Davide?"

"Perfect! Every time I can't imagine it getting any better, it does."

"That's great, Erin!"

"I know Kirk is glad you're back. He was honestly like a lost puppy."

"Kirk came over here? Oh, yeah, and I owe you for paying Maria and Antonio."

"Yes, and that was Kirk again. He asked if I knew of anything he could do for you. I told him Maria and Antonio would probably appreciate being paid." I chuckled at this. "Informed him that you pay them every Friday."

"This is normally true, except for paying them the Thursday we left. Actually, the night before, while it was on my mind, I left a couple checks where I knew Maria would see them. Remembered doing so when the payment topic came up on the day of your visit, but don't recall if I mentioned it."

"You didn't mention it, but I thought you might have done something like that. Anyway, Kirk told me he would take care of it. Are you really doing okay?"

"Really am. I'll tell you what I told Kirk. Negativity is very toxic for me and is my trigger. As long as I'm in close proximity to all that keeps me connected to myself, I'll be fine. And this includes you and everybody I feel close to. Also my writing and home. All these things are reminders of who I am, and will offset the trigger."

"Great! On that note, I'm going to head home, Ker. Will leave you to enjoy your surroundings."

"Bye, Rin, and thanks for everything."

"Don't mention it. See ya." Erin left, and I did as she said. I looked around and felt a bit famished. Thinking of the dinner Maria had prepared for me made my mouth water. I stepped inside to heat up my meal, with plans to return and eat it outside.

37

PASTTIME

It was so nice sleeping in my own bed that I slept in late. The aroma of coffee alerted me Maria had arrived, and lured me out of bed. Got myself a cup and headed out to lounge on my veranda, my favorite pastime. Was taking everything in when Kirk appeared in front of me with his arms behind his back. "Hey, babe."

"Hey, Kirk. What's going on?" I asked, suspiciously. He handed me a wrapped package. "What's this?"

"Got you a present. Hope you like it." In my excitement, I tore the paper off. It was a new laptop. "This is awesome, Kirk!" I laid it down and leaped up to hug his neck.

"Figured you were due for an upgrade."

"Probably long overdue."

"Try it out."

"All right. Also, I hear you paid Maria and Antonio for me. Thanks, and I will pay you back." I sat down, placing my legs in a pretzel formation, and pulled my gift onto my lap.

"Not necessary. I wanted to help, so end of story. I took the liberty of downloading Cathy's edits. And had Debbi draw up some preliminary cover designs, which I also downloaded. You should check them out and see what you think." Cathy had a way with words that made a story more powerful. Debbi's eye-catching designs were mesmerizing.

"Okay. I am curious to see the ideas for the cover." Kirk knelt beside me as I opened the laptop up. I pulled the designs up and took my time scrolling through them. For the first one, I liked the artwork but not the title graphics, and the second one was vice versa. I continued looking. Each had aspects I liked, but nothing fully grabbed me. The last one threw me—it had nothing but the phrase "look at me," which was not even the title of the book, but the graphics were cool. Studying this last cover, I asked, "Kirk, is this a title suggestion?"

"No, it's an instruction."

I looked over at Kirk to see he was holding a classic black velvet jewelry box. He snapped it open, revealing a diamond ring. "Well, will you marry me?"

Despite the fact I was completely surprised, I blurted out, "Yes!" With a sigh of relief, Kirk carefully placed the ring on my finger and followed with a kiss. He then stood up and began looking around.

"Where's your phone, babe?"

"Believe I left it behind the bar." I didn't even care to know why he was asking for it, probably because I was still in a bit of shock.

"Got to go now, Kerrie, but will call you later."

"Okay." I could not believe it. With my parents' marriage ending in divorce, I had never thought about marriage for myself. Lived my life by enjoying the moment, with no expectations about what was next. Might have blocked out the possibility due to a commitment phobia. Yet, when Kirk proposed, I had immediately said yes. It felt so right, that any fear present had vanished.

The ringing of my cellphone interrupted my thoughts. I thought that Kirk's promise to call later had come rather quickly. Raced over to the phone and saw it was my mother calling. Stood there frozen, just staring down at my phone. Butterflies were stirring in the pit of my stomach. "Hel-lo," I answered, with hesitation in my voice.

"Hello, Kerrie!" I was taken aback by the enthusiasm in her tone.

"Is everything all right?" I asked.

"Yes. Kirk called me, and I hear congratulations are in order." The answer I didn't care to know earlier was now very clear to me. Kirk must have sent my mother's number to his phone. "I enjoyed getting to know him when he showed up one day to collect your belongings. Wanted to call and let you know how happy I am for you. Let me know once you set a date."

"You would come?" I could not imagine why she would want to, considering her last words to me.

"Of course! Would not miss my baby girl getting married for anything."

"I'm glad! See if Hazel would like to come. If you want to."

"Okay, darling. Keep in touch."

"I will. And thanks, Mom!"

"Sure, sweetie. Will talk with you soon."

"Okay. Bye." I hung up and found myself questioning what this all meant. My mind was reeling with explanations. Then I began to wonder—could we possibly have the mother and daughter relationship I'd always wanted? That I'd craved for as a young girl? I'd always admired my mother's beauty and bubbly personality in the days before my dad left. Never knew of her struggles back then. That day in the kitchen would have been a clue, had I had the insight I did now.

Needed not to over think it. It was a huge step for my mother to even make the phone call, and that was a positive sign. Decided to just leave it at that. And then my last conversation with Kim struck me. Felt pretty certain the possibility of contact was stronger than Kim had let on but, still, it may not have happened, and there was no point in my fretting needlessly like she knew I would. Her card was my safety net, but today I didn't need to reach for it. Just wanted to bask in the moment.

Went back to the lounge chair and sat down. Stretched my arm out and looked at my ring. Could not stop gazing at it. The sight of it sparked a reflection on my life. The past, present, and future came together in my mind. Three periods of time from which life could be viewed. Inspiration struck me.

I raced inside for a notepad and pencil. Then raced back to my seat. Opened the pad and drew triangles in different places on the paper to create visuals for a metaphor, and the words followed.

Triangles can be a diagram for life. Three points representing three periods of time. The past, present, and future. Reflecting on these gives insight into who we were, who we are, and who we are to become. Can never forget our point of origin, nor can we change it, but that does not mean our lives can't change. We journey through phases of life. Each phase can give us a fresh start. A new beginning that generates hope for the possibility of a different outcome. Perhaps this is a new beginning.

ABOUT THE AUTHOR

JOANIE LUNSFORD

Joanie Lunsford is a member of Fans of Booktopia. The Booktopia events inspired her to leap into her desire to write. Being from a small town, Joanie wanted to capture the appeal of hometown closeness and bonds which transcend time and distance. Joanie lives in Georgia with her husband and two cats. This is her first novel.

CPSIA information can be obtained
at www.ICGtesting.com
Printed in the USA
FSHW011015081119
63801FS

9 781605 715025